Trouble's Child

:

Trouble's Child

:

MILDRED PITTS WALTER

:

Lothrop, Lee & Shepard Books
New York

Printed in the United States of America

First Edition

1 2 3 4 5 6 7 8 9 10

:

Library of Congress Cataloging in Publication Data
Walter, Mildred Pitts.
Trouble's child.

Summary: Martha longs to leave her island home off
the Louisiana coast and go to high school where she
can learn more than the ways of her midwife grandmother
and perhaps someday broaden the lives of the superstitious villagers.
[1. Louisiana—Fiction.   2. Grandmothers—Fiction.
3. Midwifery—Fiction.   4. Afro-Americans—Fiction]
I. Title.
PZ7.W17125Tr   1985   [Fic]   84-16387
ISBN 0-688-04214-7

:

Typography by Lynn Braswell

The folk-tale, *Strength and Power*, told by Titay is loosely based on a tale collected by Zora Neale Hurston in *Mules and Men*, first published in 1935.

:

To my friends,
Marie, Karen,
Margie, and Barbara

:

Trouble's Child

:

ONE

THE SMALL BUILDING that served as both church and school on Blue Isle was ready for the last event of the school year. Martha surveyed the room and smiled. The rough hand-hewn pews had been dusted and arranged in neat rows. Pine board walls were covered with wild azaleas; their fragrant honeysuckle sweetness filled the room. Ropes of pink, green and white crepe paper crisscrossed the ceiling beams, adding to the festive air.

The noise behind the flimsy curtain on the makeshift stage announced the arrival of the children. Martha rushed backstage and said she would tie the crepe paper bows on the girls' dresses. She could see that the teacher, Miss Boudreaux, had her hands full.

"Oh, I'm so glad you're here, Martha," Miss Boudreaux said. "I don't know what I'd do without you."

"I don't mind hepin, teacher," Martha answered softly.

Crepe paper crackled as bows were tied and flowers pinned. The noise and excitement in the place reminded Martha of the time she had stood behind the curtain, nervously awaiting her turn to appear on the stage.

Now her role in all this confusion was a different one. She listened to the teacher doing last-minute coaching and felt a tinge of sadness. She had been out of school now for a whole year, having graduated from the eighth grade. She missed studying and being with her teacher. She and Miss Boudreaux understood each other. They liked each other, that Martha knew.

The people on Blue Isle believed that a child born in a storm was born to trouble. Miss Boudreaux, aware that Martha was often taunted because she had been born during a storm, gave Martha special attention. She encouraged her to stay after school to erase the chalkboard and to talk. During Martha's last year, Miss Boudreaux let her help mark papers. When she was out of the room, Martha had been left in charge.

Now Martha stood in the middle of the confusion watching the teacher trying to control her temper as she cautioned students to keep quiet and still.

She sho pretty, Martha thought. Miss Boudreaux's green dress was lovely with her green eyes, light complexion and her long brown hair.

Noise from the front of the curtain blended with that

behind it. Martha peeped through the curtain. Titay was just walking in and Martha felt a rush of happiness. Titay was her family. She watched as Alicia, Gert and the other women gathered around Titay and felt proud to be a Dumas. *Eveybody loves m' granma,* Martha thought. Then she noticed Cora LaRue turn her head away as Titay walked by. *Well, all cept Cora.*

Ocie, a friend and former classmate, was down front with Tijai, who was called Tee. Beau, another friend, was just behind them. Martha knew that the empty space beside Beau was being saved for her. Everyone on the island expected Beau to ask for her hand.

Ocie was turned in the pew so she could talk to both Tee and Beau. Tee's dark eyes sparkled as he looked at Ocie. Everyone could tell that they were engaged to be married.

Miss Boudreaux, having somewhat quieted the children, joined Martha at the curtain.

"Tis almost full," Martha said.

"I'm glad. I just hope we do as well tonight as we did with your class last year. But your class was special. I miss y'all."

Martha felt a surge of warmth and a longing. She wanted to tell her teacher how she missed studying and how she wanted to go on to high school. As if the teacher knew what she was thinking, Miss Boudreaux said, "Martha, what are your plans?"

"Oh, teacher, I don't know. I sho would like t' go on t' high school."

"Well, there's St. Joan's. But that's fifty miles away."

Martha felt that there was little hope of her going that far. No one that she had ever heard of had gone away from Blue Isle to high school.

Miss Boudreaux smiled and said, "I just bet when I come back this fall, you will be engaged to some fine young man and ready to follow in the footsteps of that wonderful grandmother of yours."

"Oh no, teacher, don't say that. I wanna go way from this place." But Martha knew that now, because she was fourteen, the pressure on her to get married would increase. Every girl on the island was expected to announce her readiness for marriage by the age of fifteen. This announcement was made by showing a special quilt pattern. Once engaged, a round of quilting parties was given in the girl's honor.

"I wanna finish high school, yes," Martha said.

Miss Boudreaux looked at Martha with a sad smile, as if to say, getting away won't be easy. She put a hand on Martha's shoulder. "Thank you so much for helping back here. We must start now. Go out front and listen so you can tell me honestly how it was."

When Beau saw Martha, he waved. "Over here, cha." Through his happy smile she saw that quizzical frown line on his forehead. In spite of the two pox marks on his olive-tinged face—one on his nose and the other on his chin—by village standards, he was good-looking. Like Miss Boudreaux, Beau was a mulatto.

Tee greeted Martha warmly too. In Martha's eyes Tee was better looking than Beau. She liked Tee and was more at ease with him. Maybe that was because nobody expected her to marry Tee! He and Ocie were laughing and teasing, and Martha wished she could be as carefree and talkative with Beau as Ocie was with Tee.

"I shoulda knowed you'd be back there hepin the teacher," Beau said, and laughed as Martha sat beside him.

"That's Martha," Ocie said. "Still shinin up t' the teacher."

Martha, stung, tried to smile. Tee, sensing Martha's hurt, said, "One thing sho—Martha can teach rithmetic good as Miss Boudreaux."

Suddenly the place was hushed. Miss Boudreaux was before them. Martha settled to become an attentive critic.

Later that day she walked with Ocie on the dusty rutted road toward the trail that led to the Gulf of Mexico. The Gulf lay about two miles from the houses that were built high above the ground, protected from floods. The girls were on their way to join others on Blue Isle in saying goodbye to Miss Boudreaux. During the school year the teacher came to the island by boat each day.

Just as they came to the trail leading directly there, a gust of wind caught the dust up into a whirl that twisted around and around in a twirling funnel. The twisting wind raced toward Martha and trapped her in its middle, then just as quickly twirled away, high into the air.

"A devil's whirl," Ocie cried. The people believed

that a person caught in a middle of a whirl of wind would see the devil.

Martha, flustered by the wind, busily dusted her clothes and smoothed her hair.

"Did yuh see the devil?" Cora's harsh tone surprised Martha. Where had she come from so quickly?

"I had m' eyes closed," Martha answered quietly, unnerved by the sudden appearance of Cora and the question.

"Don't lie. You saw im cause that wind choosed you." Cora looked at Martha with positive contempt and hurried on.

"Did yuh really see the devil?" Ocie asked with fear in her voice.

"Wid all that dust n grit? I tole yuh, I had m' eyes closed. You don't blieve the devil's in somethin like a puff o' dust, do yuh, Ocie?"

"Yeah, and you better blieve it too."

Martha realized that she should not have asked that question. She walked behind Ocie silently on the trail that led to the Gulf.

Many of the sixty families on Blue Isle were represented at the gathering. Some had come by pirogue, a small boat hollowed out of a log. This small boat was the most commonly used transportation on the island.

Standing with the crowd, Martha wished she could have another minute alone with her teacher. She felt now more than ever that she should leave this place. Oh, why couldn't she be like others around her— happy with what she already knew? Satisfied, finished with school. No, she always wanted to know more.

With everyone shouting and waving goodbye and calling hurry back, Martha suddenly felt a rush of loneliness. As the boat moved out into the Gulf she longed to let everybody know how close she felt to Miss Boudreaux. She shouted, "Goodbye, Anita Marie."

The hush in the crowd and the frowning dismay on Titay's face let her know that she had done a terrible thing. No one on Blue Isle called the teacher by her first name in public.

Martha walked home with her grandmother, regretting the outburst. Her stomach felt weak, her hands perspired; she sensed that she had humiliated and hurt her grandmother. But she didn't know how deep that hurt was until Titay said to her, "Mat, I don't like sayin this, but you's a child bo'ned t' trouble."

TWO

MARTHA DRESSED hurriedly. She wanted to be out of the house before her grandmother was up and about. Ocie would be waiting, ready for them to begin hanging the stretched frame for Ocie's final quilting party. Even before Ocie was fourteen she had already shown her quilt pattern. Tee had bid for and won her hand. Many quilting parties had been held for Ocie and for weeks now the island had buzzed with preparations for her wedding.

Five quilts had been finished. Ocie and her mother had embroidered pillowcases and other linens. Now the final quilting party would be held at the home of Gert, Ocie's mother-in-law to be.

Children passed Martha's house on their way to pick

mayhaws, the small applelike fruit that made fragrant jelly. Their talk, their laughter and the clicking of sticks to startle snakes reminded Martha of the times she and her friends had done the same.

"Mat," Titay called. "Where you at?"

Oh no, Martha thought. "I'm heah, Granma."

"We gonna git that sassfras tday, yes?"

Martha felt her lips pouting. *Why she choose tday t' clect sassfras?* "Granma," she said, "Ocie want me t' hep er git ready fuh the party."

"You gon go wid me."

Martha knew that her grandmother was still upset with her for calling the teacher by her first name. She did not say more. *Never git t' do what I wanna do.*

Before long, armed with a stick to drive away snakes, Martha walked behind her grandmother on the trail that would take them from the Gulf, deep into the woods. She carried their large handwoven basket on her head.

The commissary, the social center for the 250 people on the island, was near this trail. This small store was owned by a mulatto, Ovide. With its weather-bleached siding, the commissary looked like other houses on the island except for its roof. Made of tin, the roof gleamed in the midst of houses covered with paper, seamed with tar.

Here mail was delivered. Men met to talk and women visited together while they waited for sugar, flour, lard and cane syrup from barrels placed around the room. They exchanged recipes and dress patterns and often haggled with Ovide about the price of cotton calico. But bargaining rarely changed the price, for there were no other stores.

Martha waited impatiently as Titay, having decided to order wire for a new clothesline, disappeared into the commissary.

Just then Ocie walked up. "Where you go, cha?" she called to Martha. "Thought you hepin me tday."

Martha's face burned. "Granma still upset wid me. Gotta go wid her."

"How come yuh didn't tell er you's hepin fix fuh the party?"

Titay reappeared and walked on toward the trail. Martha lowered her voice. "I did. But you know her. I'll come soon as we git back, yes."

Ocie shrugged and went into the commissary, leaving Martha hurt and disappointed.

Martha caught up with her grandmother, who moved with a slow but steady pace. Titay was old. Her body appeared frail. Her hair was white like the frothy foam of waves; but her voice was strong, her hands steady and her mind clear. She was the island's midwife and the people looked to her for health care and wisdom.

Soon they came to the place where they often gathered sassafras bark, roots and leaves. The leaves were ground into a seasoning called filé for use in gumbo, a seafood soup. The root bark made delicious tea that some people on the island drank as a tonic.

Usually Martha was happy in the woods listening to the birds, smelling magnolia blossoms and carefully handling delicate touch-me-not flowers. When she was younger, she often left Titay to chase butterflies and to play hide-and-seek with shadows of the trees. In the woods among green and growing things she could forget she was the granddaughter of the island's caretaker. There Titay was *her* grandmother, telling her stories about the animals and other wonderful things in the woods. But today her mind was not on picking leaves. She wanted to be away from the woods with Ocie, sharing the excitement of the quilting preparations.

"C'mon, girl, fill yo basket. Where yo mind?" Titay called.

Martha said nothing but speeded up the collection of the bright green leaves. She picked easily, moving closer and closer to Titay.

Suddenly she saw something in the underbrush near her grandmother. For a moment she couldn't breathe; she wanted to shout, but she knew Titay must not be startled into making a sudden move. Martha rattled the bushes with her stick.

"Oh, I didn't see it, no!" Titay cried as the snake slithered away.

Martha shivered. Was Titay getting careless, or was her grandmother losing her eyesight? Martha was tempted to insist that they go right home, but she knew her grandmother would not think of leaving. She carefully beat the bush before starting to pick again.

The sun had moved toward the middle of the sky when Martha and Titay left the woods. At home they found a pail of mayhaws the children had left at their door. Martha felt a surge of anger and disappointment. Helping to preserve mayhaws would delay her even more.

Titay was delighted. She looked at Martha. "Why you poutin?"

"Granma, I promised Ocie . . ."

"Yuh go when I say go. Now go head n p'pare them leaves; I'll take care the mayhaws."

Martha worked fast. She still wanted to have time to see if everything was ready for Ocie's party.

"Now you can scald them jars fuh this jelly," Titay said.

"Aw, Granma." If only she hadn't blurted out the teacher's first name. She wished she could tell Titay that she was going anyway. But she wouldn't dare. No one talked back to the elderly, and especially not to Titay.

"When yuh learn not t' talk so much, I can let yuh go round the women thout me." Titay went about her work. Martha sullenly did the jars.

Finally Titay said, "Now you go. But I want you t' member this: tis the shallow brook that babbles and tis still water that runs deep."

By the time Martha arrived the party was well underway. The women had already made three rolls of the quilt and their fingers were moving rapidly, forming the tiny stitches that made the pattern stand out so beautifully.

"Hey, Mat, c'mon in heah and start in threadin these needles," Alicia called.

"Look at er. Don't she look good?" Gert said.

"Like new money. I swear the girl done growed like overnight," Cam said.

"She useta be a cute lil girl wid a cute lil figger sayin, stand back, boys, til I git a lil bigger," Ocie said. "But she can't say that no mo. She's a cute girl wid a cute figger, step up, boys, cause she ain't gon git no bigger."

All the women laughed and Gert said "Yeah, and Beau better stop his lollygaggin round heah, cause Mat's gon be ready soon, ahn, Mat?"

Martha's feeling of ease slipped away.

"Tell us, Mat, when you gon show yo patten? Tis bout time, yes?" Cora LaRue asked.

"Le's git Ocie married first." She didn't want to talk about marriage to Beau, or to anyone, especially in front of Cora LaRue. So Martha said, "Ocie, le's see yo weddin dress patten."

Ocie was pleased to show her material and pattern. Both were simple, but nice. She had chosen soft white calico with fine lace and tiny buttons. It would be a dress that could be worn many times after the wedding to parties and festivals.

The women settled to quilting and their talk turned to prices at the commissary. Then they talked about plans for the fishing festival, the biggest event on the island, which came every year at the end of summer. Finally their conversation turned to their children.

"Say, Cam, you's lookin mighty pretty round heah," Cora said. "Yo skin like velvet. You ain't in child way agin, no?"

There was deep silence broken by Cam's uneasy giggle. She covered her mouth to hide a missing front tooth. "Ah, Miss Cora, leave me lone."

Martha lowered her eyes, trying to relieve the hurt she felt for Cam. Only a few days ago, Cam had come to visit Titay, upset because she felt she was expecting another child. It would be her fifth, and her youngest was only nine months old. She and Titay had talked for a long time. When Cam left, Titay was silent, and Martha knew her grandmother faced a problem she could not solve.

Just then Tee came through the door. "Look who I brung," he said, ushering Titay into the room. Everyone applauded. Cora said, "You jus in time t' tell us bout Cam."

Titay gave Cam a quick look, then turned to Cora. "What's t' tell?"

"Aw now, Miss Titay, look at er. She's too pretty. You mus know there'll be a new baby round heah soon, yes?"

Everyone knew that Cora wanted to take Titay's place as the island midwife and caretaker, but the women were afraid of her. It was rumored that she practiced hoodoo. Her question now was meant to put Titay on the spot.

The women were quiet as Cora kept her angry eyes on Titay. In that throbbing moment, Martha wondered how Titay would answer.

"Ah," Titay said. "That need no word from me, no. If it be so, we'll know sooner or later, ahn?" She moved to place a hand on Cam's shoulder.

Martha caught Cam's eye and responded to her smile.

Cora's anger chilled the room, but Titay calmly took her place at the quilting frame to do the work in the center of the final roll.

Martha smiled again. Even if Titay's eyes were failing, she still made the neatest, most even stitches, twelve within an inch.

Just as the frame was being taken down, the men began to arrive. Soon the party moved outside and shouts went up for Ocie and Tee to do the courting dance. Drumbeats and hand-clapping set the rhythm. Ocie stood still, marking time to the music, while Tee did steps that moved from the simple to the most difficult.

Tee strutted on his toes, moving his shoulders, neck, arms and head. Ocie teased with her eyes and smile while she stood in place, keeping time to the beat. The tempo increased and Tee's whole body caught the music.

Martha, fired by the music and movements, clapped and urged the dancers on.

After the courting dance everyone was ready for cake and lemonade. As they settled and were served, the men began to swap tall tales. The women listened and laughed. Only Cora was bold enough to add a story of her own and sip the elderberry wine that Tee's father brought out for the men to sample.

Martha sat on the ground, close to Titay, watching, listening and laughing at the stories. She felt at home, but with an uneasiness hard for her to explain. It was like moving down a smooth, endless road without a single curve. She looked up at Titay and said, "I'm ready t' go, Granma, when you ready." Then she leaned her head on Titay's knee and listened to the laughter.

THREE

THE GULF was calm, and the murmur of the waves seemed to be whispering a blessing on the day of Ocie's wedding. Martha slept late. When she awoke, the sun was hot in a cloudless sky.

She lay in bed wondering how she would fill her days now. She wouldn't have Ocie. With Tee in her life, Ocie would have much more in common with the married women.

Oh, if only she could leave this place. She wished she had talked more to the teacher, had tried to create some plans. But going to high school would mean being away from home for months. Suddenly she recalled that snake sliding off into the brush. *Who'd look after Granma? Wish I had a big family.*

Martha had never known her mother. Her father, Titay's youngest son, had drowned in the Gulf before she was five years old. He was now only a faint memory. Then she thought, *There's Beau and gittin married.* But she quickly put that out of her mind.

If only there was someone who understood her. She was only fourteen, and her life was already over. *Silly!* There was still a lot to do. There was the fishing festival only two months away. *Who's gon lead em dancin down t' the sea? Titay, probly. Hard t' blieve Granma so old. She's led that dancin since I can member.*

The church bell rang.

Martha was still in bed when Titay called, "You ready in there?"

"I'm comin, but you go on, Granma." She was glad now that she had decided to wear the pale blue voile dress that had belonged to her mother. Though the sheer cotton was more than fourteen years old, it was still lovely and fitted her just right. She wished she had a wide, soft straw hat like the one the teacher wore in the sun. Titay's parasol would have to do.

The green of the trees was deep and solid and shining under the brilliant silver sky. Stepping lively on the trail, Martha admired her tall lean shadow, sheltered by the small parasol. As she walked along enjoying the sounds and fervor of her island, she forgot that moments before she had thought her life over.

Near Ocie's house Martha's excitement increased. All of Ocie's family were getting in line for the wedding march to the church. Suddenly Martha wished she had gone earlier to see if her friend needed anything: something borrowed, maybe. Then she saw Ocie with her father. Ocie looked nervous, but pretty.

From a distance Martha watched the march begin, knowing she had plenty of time. Ocie and her family would take the long route to the church that passed many houses. Anyone unable to attend the ceremony could see the bride and wish her happiness.

The church was already crowded when Martha arrived. Titay was in a place right down front. With a magnolia blossom in her hair, she looked prouder than the parents. After all, she had delivered both Tee and Ocie, which gave her special claim. Martha was happy there was still a seat in the back pew.

Soon the bridal party arrived. Ocie walked through the church followed by all of her family. She no longer looked nervous. Now she was beaming. Smiling shyly at Tee as he waited with his family behind him, she leaned toward him and lost her balance. Tee caught her and hugged her close. There were sounds of appreciation for the beauty of the scene.

"Who gi'e this woman in marriage?" The preacher's voice boomed. The ceremony was underway.

There was a long silence. Ocie's father had tears in his eyes. *What he thinkin?* Ocie was his only daughter and she was young. Just fifteen.

When Ocie's father couldn't speak, her mother spoke up and said, "I do."

Suddenly Martha could not hold back her tears. Who would answer for her? *I ain't got nobody but Titay. We can't even make a weddin party.* She swallowed again and again to stifle her sobs.

But weddings are for fun, and Ocie's was well planned for just that. Her father came alive as he and

Ocie's brothers played never-ending music. There was loud talk and laughter as people enjoyed the many dishes. Just as Tee's father was the island's best fisherman, his mother was the finest cook. There were fresh shrimp, tubs of crawfish, lots of Gert's gumbo and rice and many delicious cakes, puddings and pies.

The celebration lasted far into the night with everyone dancing, including Titay. Martha, catching the rhythm of the drums, rocked the party with her movements. There were whispers: "She will take Titay's place, sho, and lead the festival."

Martha woke drenched. Her little room seemed without air. She got out of bed and was surprised to find no sun. A heavy fog hung over the island. The quiet frightened her until she realized that it was already noon, dinnertime.

Titay was making her rounds visiting the sick. Martha went into the kitchen feeling drained by the heat. Titay had left a covered plate on the table. Curious, Martha lifted the cover. Cake! Leftovers from Ocie's wedding. She could not resist—one piece, then two. The cake made her thirsty.

She went outside to fill the water pail, but it was so hot, she sat under the pump letting the water stream over her. Then she drank and drank. It was a great effort to move. Before she had changed her dripping clothes, she was hot again. Feeling worn, she decided to go back to bed.

When she awoke, the fog had gone; the sinking sun left the sky aglow.

"What'd you do tday? You ain't even swept the flo, no?" Titay was preparing supper.

"It be too hot, Granma." Martha got busy to help finish the meal. They ate in silence, and while Martha put food away and washed the dishes, Titay went to sit outside. Soon Martha smelled the smoke from rags set out to smolder and keep mosquitoes away. Voices of people who came for advice or just to talk briefly with Titay drifted to her.

Before she had finished the dishes, Titay called in the voice she always used to summon Martha for serious talk. "Mat, come heah."

Martha stood in the doorway.

"C'mon, sit, girl."

The smoke curled up and spread out, stinging Martha's eyes and nose. There was silence between them.

"Ocie had good weddin, yes?" Titay finally said.

"Eveybody had good time, yes. Know I did."

"They liked yo dancin. They all say how good you look and what woman you is now. So I think tis time fo you t' start thinkin bout yo life work. I'm old, Mat. Done kept the way o' this island. I gather herbs, wait on the sick. Peoples look t' me fo midwifin. I hope yuh ready t' take m' place."

The warm sticky sweat that had bothered Martha all day suddenly chilled. She shivered.

"You mus git ready fuh yo quiltin. I'll vite the whole island and show yo patten. They'll know yo hand's out fuh marryin."

Martha felt the muscles tighten in her throat. She sucked in her breath, fighting the feeling of suffocation. Across the way in the dark, small houses stood in rows. The light of the stars was strong and bright. The night was filled with sounds, and with the smells of flowers, of the Gulf and of wet and dry things. Suddenly she felt a surge of love for this place.

She longed to tell her grandmother that she didn't want to be married, not now. There was no one on Blue Isle she wanted as a husband. But how could she say she would not have quilting parties, would not marry? She knew of no one who had not.

Titay went on. "You'll like yo patten. I dreamed this one befo you's bo'ned. I see this plain piece wid five rings in the cener locked t' one nother, making a design in the middle o' the rings. Twas so clear that I knowed it would make a beautiful quilt patten. And I prayed fuh a girl chile t' come in this family. God blessed me only wid sons. And they all been gift t' the Gulf. Oh Mat, tis you that keep me goin. I'll teach you so you can take m' place and keep the way."

"But Granma . . . can't we wait awhile?"

"Why wait, girl?"

"Cause, Granma. I thought . . . well, I'm thinkin . . . I wanna go way."

"Go way where?" Titay snapped.

"T' high school, mebbe."

"You done finish school. Now you learn from me. We gather herbs and seaweed. We make the rounds, visit the sick. I'll learn yuh all you need know."

A voice came out of the darkness. "Titay, we smell

yo smoke way yonder, and we yearn fuh yo talk." It was Alicia.

"Can we sit wid y'all?" Gert asked.

"Welcome," Titay said.

"Cora by yo house, yes?" Gert asked.

"Cora LaRue?" Titay was surprised. "No, not heah, no."

"We jus seen er, yes. She move quick thout sayin the time o' day t' us," Gert said.

"Not heah, no. Passin, mebbe. Come, sit." Titay seemed glad that they had come.

Martha *was* glad. They gave her time. As soon as the women started talking about children, eggs and chickens, she excused herself.

She went to her small room and lay on her bed, and her grandmother's words disturbed her more and more. *Yo hand's out for marryin . . . I'll teach yuh . . . we make the rounds . . . keep the way of the island.*

No, no, no, Martha thought. She had to get away. But to where? She had never been off the island and she had no one but Titay. She had known that Titay depended upon her to become the midwife long before the words were spoken, but now Titay's hopes were stated and could not be ignored. If she didn't become the midwife, Cora would.

Slowly Martha undressed in the darkness and got into bed. The sound of the Gulf in the distance did not soothe her.

FOUR

"MAT, le's git a early start," Titay called.
Martha got up and opened the wooden
shutter to her small window. It was just
before dawn. The morning star, big and bright, seemed
to hang close to earth, far from the sky. The urge to lie
down again tugged at her, but she sat on the bed and
slowly put on her clothes.

"We gather seaweed tday," Titay said, handing
Martha a basket and small rakes.

At the Gulf, Martha walked close to Titay along the
shore with the basket on her head. She took Titay's
arm to give support and suddenly felt as if she had become the woman and Titay the girl. For a moment, a
love for her grandmother filled her. Then Titay's words

came to her again: *Take m' place and keep the way*, and Martha felt afraid.

Martha wondered how she could ever take her grandmother's place in the hearts of the people. Titay was wise and knew so much. Martha longed to open up and tell Titay about her doubts, about the pain she felt when people said that she was born to trouble. She wanted to say that she could never be like Alicia and Gert. Not like Ocie. Not even like Titay. Words rushed around in her head as she raked in silence, filling her basket, carefully avoiding dead and decaying weeds.

The sun burned through the fog. Waves caught the light, rushing to the shore with caps of white foam. Still raking carefully, Martha thought of the fishing festival, just a month away. She looked at her grandmother, who was raking with great energy, and shouted over the sound of the Gulf, "Granma, yuh think they meant it when they say I make good leader fuh the festival?"

Titay smiled. "They know good dancer when they see one."

Joy sounded in Martha's voice when she said, "So yuh think so, ahn?"

"I think so, yes."

When the basket was filled, they started back. People were now up and about. Beau and other Spanish moss pickers with long poles and gunny sacks moved on the trail that led deep into the woods. Smoke rose from many chimneys. Breakfast was over, and now the women were beginning preparations for the noonday meal.

On the way back Martha and Titay saw Ocie and Tee. They had a three-room house like most on the island: one room followed the other from front to back. Tee was sitting on the steps of the high porch while Ocie stood in the door talking to him.

"Hey, cha," Ocie called to Martha. "C'mon, you n Titay."

"I'm weary, but Mat'll come," Titay said.

Martha felt ashamed that she had not visited her friends since they had settled. Each day had given her a new excuse. She placed the basket near the front steps and plopped down near Tee, but one step lower. Ocie joined them and sat beside her husband.

"Long time no see you, no. Why ain't yuh come, cha?"

"Busy. Titay be workin me hard, yes."

"I hear yuh mebbe leavin, no?" Ocie asked.

Martha looked up, surprised. "Who say so?"

"Tis round. They say you won't lead the fishin festival cause you gon go way."

"I don't know who tole yuh that."

"Aw, come on. You always thought you better'n us."

Martha, stunned, could not speak.

"Why you say that, Cie?" Tee asked. "She never done that round me."

"She put on airs round teacher, specially when she take teacher's place, yes."

Martha looked at Ocie, surprised at the attack. Was Ocie just guessing that she wanted to go away? *Sholy I ain't tole er that and fogot it. No,* Martha thought. She had never told anyone except Titay. Who did Titay tell? Finally she said to Ocie, "I don't know what you mean, better'n y'all." She picked up her basket and started to leave.

"Don't go, cha. I was only kiddin, honest. But I did heah you gon go way, though."

"Don't bring gossip less you name the sender. Good day, y'all."

"Wait, I'll carry yo basket," Tee said.

They walked along in silence, Martha trying to control the feeling of betrayal. Who could be saying that she would leave before the festival? *And Ocie, callin erself m' friend and spreadin mess.*

Finally Tee said, "Don't be shamed if you wanna leave this place. I did one time too. I yearn now, but no use fuh me. Fuh you, yes."

"But who say sich: I think mahself better?"

"Women talk. But pay no mind t' that. You mebbe too good fuh heah, no? I think, mebbe, yes. And if you git a chance, go. It make you no better, no worse'n us, no."

Martha fought back the tears. She was grateful that someone understood, but she didn't know what to say, so she said nothing.

When they arrived at her house Tee set the basket inside. He looked at her with a broad grin, then left. She knew he understood her silence, and for that her gratitude expanded.

FIVE

SUMMER MOVED toward fall. Martha kept her thoughts to herself and joined Titay on the rounds to visit the sick and to gather herbs. Each morning she promised herself to speak to Titay about the rumor that she was leaving, but each night she could not find the courage to do so.

Finally one morning before they started on their rounds, Martha said, "Granma, I wanna talk t' yuh."

"Tis bout time. You gotta cide on a dress fuh the festival. You leadin the dance, yes?"

"Granma, I don't think they really want me."

"Who say sich?"

Surely her grandmother had heard the gossip. Why was she pretending not to know what was going on? Martha wanted to cry out, You tole that I wanna go way, but she couldn't bring herself to say that to her grandmother. "I'll think bout a dress," she said.

As they made the rounds, Martha listened. Although the women never said anything in her presence, Martha felt that they watched her suspiciously. In silence she went about her work. She prepared cayenne leaves to burn slowly in fetid rooms to fumigate and purify the air; she concocted tea for colicky babies; she watched the ritual of preparing bodies for burial. She went her way as though unaware of the gossip of the women.

Three days before the fishing festival Titay called to Martha in a firm voice, "Come heah!"

Before Martha could ask why, Titay shouted, "How come yuh say you won't lead festival cause you gon go way?"

Martha, surprised by the tone, could not answer.

"Why?"

Martha stared at the floor.

"Heah I am blievin you's a good woman, ready t' take m' place cause yo work been good. I see in yuh the makin o' a strong midwife, n bhind m' back you go n say yuh leavin, yes?"

Martha looked at her grandmother in disbelief. "I didn't say that, no, Granma."

"Then who did? Why yuh lie, Mat?"

"Please, Granma, I didn't."

"Then *who*?" Titay shouted.

"I don't know, less it be you!"

"You dare call me liar?"

It was as though her grandmother's words had banished her to hell's fire. "Oh no, Granma," she cried. Shocked at her thoughts and behavior, Martha rushed from the house and fled down the path to the Gulf.

The sound of the waves compounded her fear and shame. She felt as if her grandmother was playing games with her. Titay must have told.

Martha watched the waves, knowing that she had done a terrible thing to suggest that Titay had lied. Then she wished Titay had slapped her face. She would feel purged, cleansed. But Titay wouldn't. Now there would be a terrible silence between them and that would be far worse than a licking.

Though the sun sank and twilight was almost purple, Martha still lingered at the edge of the Gulf. Then it was dark. She hurried on the path.

In the center of the island women were gathered under the chinaberry tree, laughing and talking. As she passed they became quiet. In the dark she could feel their hostile stares.

She found the door to her grandmother's room closed, which meant that Titay was deep in meditation, *communin*. Martha wanted to cry out, I'm home, Granma, but she was too ashamed. She went quickly, quietly to her room.

Hand-clapping to the beat of the music rang throughout the island. The fishing festival was underway. Martha paced up and down the room, her hands over her ears, trying to close out the merrymaking. Her long, ruffled white gauze skirt and full-sleeved blouse were perfect for a leader of the dance. Her hair, braided in plaits with many colorful beads, fell to her shoulders. If only she felt as lovely as she looked.

She thought of the past days and the silence between her and her grandmother. She had wanted to ask for forgiveness and to try to probe with Titay into the reasons why someone would want to play that horrible trick on them. But she could not break through Titay's stony silence. Titay acted as though Martha did not exist.

Martha went to stand in the front door of the house. The music taunted her. *Cora will lead. Cora LaRue! Oh no,* she thought. That's exactly what Cora wanted, to take the dancers to the sea. *Cora by yo house, yes? ... We jus seen er ... She move quick thout sayin the time o' day ...* Gert's words flashed into Martha's mind.

Suddenly she dashed from the house tying an emerald green scarf around her waist as she ran. Her heartbeat quickened with her footsteps.

As she came to the square, shouts from the crowd urged a dancer on. Dust rose as a gold and green skirt thrashed the air. Cora danced wildly, alone in the center of the circle. Martha was too late. *So Cora will lead em,* she thought, stopping on the edge of the circle. Then to her surprise, the crowd opened to include her, and in that moment Cora's rhythm was broken.

Cora flashed an angry look at Martha, encouraged the musicians and started a new dance.

Martha suddenly felt shy. She looked around the circle. Ocie was standing between her husband and Beau. Both men were wearing the simple white cotton pants and blousy shirts of the fishermen, even though Tee was the only one going on the voyage. Beau smiled and winked at Martha. Martha lowered her eyes. *Wish I liked im cause he sho act like I'm his heartstring.*

A shout came from the crowd. "Dance, Martha!"

Martha's shyness returned and she didn't know what to do. She felt the urge to respond, but she couldn't even clap her hands to the music.

Then Tee shouted, "G'on, Martha, shake a leg, girl!" Ocie, Beau and others joined in, and the rhythm became, "Dance, Martha, dance."

Cora glared at Martha, stamped her foot angrily and pushed through to the edge of the circle.

I'll show er, Martha thought. She closed her eyes, swayed to the music, raised her arms and snapped her fingers. Her movement was like a smoldering fire that bursts into flame and leaps to consume all in its way. Martha danced.

Later, as everybody danced, lost in the music, Titay shouted, "Le's move t' the sea."

Martha took the scarf from around her waist and waved it high as she led them all. With scarves from their waists and heads as banners, the women danced with Martha to the sea.

On the shore, the fishermen kissed the women and children. Martha glowed with the excitement of the moment. She was surprised when Tee stooped to kiss her forehead and whispered, "Don't wait heah too long."

She wanted badly to embrace him, but that was forbidden, so she smiled and said, "You diffunt, yuh know?" That was their goodbye as he moved to go aboard the fishing boat.

Whispering winds and sunlit waves urged the fishermen on their way. Beau swam alongside the boat with the men and boys who were remaining in the village. The women on the woodland shore sang and waved their flowing scarves.

Titay placed her hands on Martha's shoulders and drew Martha to her. Martha trembled. Her throat felt closed as she fought back the tears. For a moment she could not speak. Then she said, "Fuhgi me, Granma. I know now twas Cora who started it all."

"Tis all over now. But I knowed you'd come t' yo senses and be the woman t' take m' place."

Martha moved, reluctantly, out of Titay's arms. Titay joyfully rejoined the women on the shore.

Martha now stood alone, apart from the shouting crowd. She watched the boat become a dark speck and disappear. Tee's whispered caution and Titay's words battled in her mind. Twisting her scarf, she felt afraid. Alone. How could she ever leave Blue Isle?

SIX

HOWLING WIND and clapping thunder woke Martha. Lightning flashed, as she jumped out of bed and ran to the front of the house. Titay was already up, preparing for the storm watch. Martha helped to fill oil lamps, secure windows and pad doors with worn quilts. She waited with a frown on her face as Titay busied herself covering the mirror.

Her grandmother believed that mirrors drew lightning and that they also had to be covered when someone died. Martha doubted this. *Miss Boudreaux say mirrors do nothin but reflec. Like light on water.*

Over the wind, voices and loud knocking sounded. "Titay, Titay, let us in." A group of women had come.

As a gust of wind rushed through the open door and put out the lamp, a flash of lightning lit the room. In that flash, Martha saw a flickering vision of Ocie and other women, struggling to close the door.

Then the storm hit. Rain slashed upon the house. The rain, the wind and the Gulf joined in a terrifying noise. Martha saw her grandmother's hand tremble as she lit the lamp.

Finally the women and their frightened children settled around the room: some on the floor, some on chairs. No one spoke, but the women's eyes and their movements told that they too were afraid. They crossed themselves: touched forehead, breast, left and right shoulders with the tips of the fingers and thumb of the right hand. Lips moved in silent prayer for the men at sea. Martha sat apart from the women, in a corner, wondering what they were thinking. She wished Ocie had sat close to her.

Ocie sat near her mother-in-law, Gert, with her legs crossed, her elbow on her knee, chin firmly in her hand. She patted one foot as the other swung in and out with a quick rhythm: in and out, in and out. Her eyes closed, her face tense, she looked old and more frightened than any of the other women.

Suddenly Ocie fell upon Gert and cried out. "Tee won't come back from the Gulf, I know."

"Talk only that you know, cha. What yuh mean, he won't come back?" Gert asked, enfolding Ocie in her arms.

"He made me promise not t' tell. But he was bo'ned gift t' the Gulf. He got a lil hole at the top o' the ear. Can't hardly see it, but tis there."

Gert cried out. "He got no hole in is ear, no."

All the women talked at once, for they believed that a person with a small hole in the ear was sure to die of drowning.

"But he do, yes. And he know it all the time," Ocie cried.

"But I bo'ned the boy and I never seen it. Titay, you seen im; did he have what she say?"

"Calm yoself. I see nothin like that on Tee. But a wife see what none other don't see."

Wind swooped around the house and the lamp went out. Lightning played around the room; thunder crashed and rolled. Children screamed in the darkness. Then there was silence as Titay relit the lamp. She moved it to the floor and said, "Come, le's sit round the light."

They all huddled together. Martha sat with eyes down, unable to look at Ocie, who was crying softly now.

"Le's not chase trouble," Titay said softly. "Wolf scratchin at the door don't always git in."

There was a lull in the wind, and the quiet in the room was overwhelming.

"Talk t' us, Titay," one of the women said.

"Tell us a story," another asked.

What story would she tell? Would she tell about the stormy night Martha was born? Martha hoped not. She hated to be reminded of it.

"Tell how the rattler come t' git its rattlers," someone said.

"No, Miss Titay, tell bout how men got strength and women got power," Cam pleaded.

Titay folded her arms and looked at each one in the room. Then, in her warm storytelling voice, she began.

: :

"Once on a time when the land had mo fruit, mo fish and mo fowl than the peoples could eat, man and woman lived tgether equal. Woman was strong as man and never had t' take low. When they had a fight, woman could win as often as man could.

Then one day woman beat man so bad, he got mad and went up t' see the Lawd. 'Lawd, please gimme strength so I can put that woman in er place.'

The Lawd gi'e the man mo strength. Soon as he got t' the house, he commence bossin the woman and pushin er round. They got t' fightin. Oh, she fought like a tiger, but he got the best of er. She caught er wind and went at im again. But on the third time he put the wood on er back and the water on er face. She knowed she was whupped.

Woman was so hurt, she went up t' the Lawd. 'Lawd, how come yuh gi'e man mo strength?'

'Cause he ast fuh it,' the Lawd said.

'Well, you oughta see how he actin, bossin me round. You oughta gi'e me mo strength.'

'I can't gi'e you mo strength cause I gi'ed it t' man. And what I gi'e, I don't take back.'

Woman was so mad, she went straight t' the devil and told im what had happened.

'Don't be so upset, woman. Git the frown off yo face and go on back and tell the Lawd t' gi'e yuh that bunch o' keys on his mantle. Bring em back heah t' me and I'll tell yuh how t' use em.'

Sho nuff the keys was there and the woman got em. She was tired o' goin back n forth tween the Lawd and the devil, but she had t' do somethin t' live wid that man. So she went on back t' the devil.

There was three keys on that bunch. The devil took the keys and said, 'Now this first key is t' the kitchen. Man sho favors his food. This second key is t' the bedroom. He can't do thout sleep. And this third key is t' the cradle. He loves his generations. Now I want you t' lock them three doors and don't open em til he say he gon use his strength fuh yo good and yo desire.'

Woman went home and locked the doors. The man come and found he couldn't git in. 'Who locked this door?'

'Me. The Lawd gi'ed me the keys.'

The man got mad, but the woman didn't care. She ain't unlock nothin.

Things got so bad the man had t' go back up t' the Lawd. 'Lawd, how come you gi'e that woman them keys?'

'Cause she ast fuh em. I gi'ed em t' er and the devil showed er how t' use em.'

'Please gimme some jus like em so she can't be in control.'

'What I gi'e, I don't take back. Woman got the keys.'

Man went on back home. 'Woman, le's share this thing: you have mo strength sometime and I have the keys sometime.'

'Got t' think bout that.' Woman went to scuss it wid the devil.

'No, don't you share nothin. Let im keep mo strength, and you keep yo keys. That's power.'

So t' this day, man got mo strength, and woman got mo power."

: :

There was laughter and Martha felt the calm that touched them all. She could never replace her grandmother in the hearts of the people.

The storm passed. From her back door Martha watched the dark water swirl beneath her. As far as she could see, the land was flooded. Water and sky were the same dark color. Trees sagged with heavy moss. The unpainted houses that a few days ago were bleached white by the sun were now black, drenched with rain.

Martha felt numb, swollen with a lump in her chest that would not go away. They had waited. Now they were sure; all but two of the fishermen were safe. One of Alicia's cousins had been swept overboard during the storm and Tee had tried to save him. They both had drowned. Why Tee?

Martha looked out over the Louisiana land of bayous, rivers, snakes and cypress where she had been born and where her ancestors had been slaves. Not far away a raccoon swam by. His dark eyes and nose floated above the water while his paws felt for frogs and shellfish below. Except for the sound of the swirling water, the earth was silent.

The tolling church bell, calling the people to come

and sit all night with the families of the dead, made her more miserable. Martha knew that she and Titay would go, but in her own grief for Tee, Martha did not want to face Ocie and Gert. She wanted to be alone.

Martha glanced at her grandmother. Titay stood at the stove, her attention on the shrimp and rice dish she was preparing to take to the wake. She seemed so small, but relaxed in a way that shut her off from Martha and the world.

What was Titay thinking now? Her husband, Martha's grandfather, had gone down into the Gulf; her son, Martha's father, had gone by way of a storm. Titay knew well the wind and the towering dark waves. She had made many gifts to the Gulf of Mexico.

Martha turned again to the swirling water. Did Titay and the people on the island know something that she could not fathom? Could Tee have been born to drown? If so, then she was born to trouble. Was she also evil? Could she become like Cora LaRue? Once she and Ocie had slipped into Cora's house. It frightened her now to think of the jars and bottles with snakes, spiders, frogs, lizards and unknown things. Some animals were in water, some were turning to dust. People said Cora made her hoodoo potions from those. . . .

"Girl," Titay called. "Time t' git ready."

When she had put on her heavy rubber boots to guard against snakes that might still lurk in the flood water, she said to Titay, "Lemme help yuh, Granma."

She tied the string of Titay's oilskin hat and helped

Titay into her coat. Then they stood in the doorway to wait.

The dull gray of evening was turning quickly to deep purple, and night sounds filled the air. Crickets chirped. Frogs answered one another in a battle of sounds. Lightning bugs blinked pinpoint sparks in the darkness.

Soon Martha heard singing as the men and women waded toward them carrying torches made of tree branches. The fire-lights reflected on the water, brightening the night.

Beau came to help Titay and Martha. Martha refused his hand and quickly stepped down into the swirling water. She was so involved with her thoughts that she didn't sing as she marched along to the church. The small building was filled with friends and families of Tee and Alicia's cousin. Titay embraced the women and kissed the babies.

The singing kept up, one song after another. There was hand-clapping and foot-stamping, but Martha still felt numb. Her hands sweated, and her heart felt crowded in her chest. Her eyes were hot and dry.

Around midnight all became still. Everyone waited and listened. Right at twelve a rooster crowed. Then another farther away, and still another. When the round of cock crowing ended, the wife of Alicia's cousin stood and talked about her husband. The whole family took turns, with Alicia talking last. Then it was Ocie's turn. She stood and for a long time she trembled, and Martha thought she would fall. But finally

Ocie tried to speak. Her voice sounded full of tears. Beau went to stand beside her. Then she straightened her shoulders and said in a clear voice, "I speak fuh m' husband, Tijai. He was a good man. Not easy scared, and strong."

Martha's mind was full of Tee. He *was* good. Kind and thoughtful. Different from the others. Was he different because he was a born gift to the Gulf? Like she was different because she was born in a storm? *No,* Martha thought. If Tee believed that, he would have been afraid of water. Instead he tried to defy the Gulf and save a life. Not only that, he had understood her longings. He had dared to tell her to leave the island. He had not thought her strange. Martha felt the pain of having no one to talk to now—no one who understood.

Day dawned. The people left the church and moved toward the Gulf for the burial rites. They waded in shallow flood water, down to the muddy shore. The Gulf was calmer now. Brown waves washed in and out with the frying sound of foam.

The people spread out in a straight line and sang against the rhythm of the waves. Titay came forward slowly, frail. Her voice was clear, but soft. "We always take outta the Gulf its best—seaweed, fish, shrimps and crabs." Then she spoke louder. "The Gulf now quest our best. We spond with human power in this act o' makin gifts. We gi'e in grief, but with know'n joy that the Gulf'll gi'e always mo'n it take. The Gulf is generous."

Then the two wives came forward, the oldest first, and cast pebbles upon a receding wave. Ocie, casting her pebbles, said, "T' the mighty Gulf, I gi'e m' husband, Tijai Mouton." Then there was loud crying and moaning as the waves washed the gifts out to the deep.

Martha lingered alone on the shore, remembering the women's tears. She paced back and forth, wondering if she could ever do what Tee had said she should. Now she wished she had said something else to him that would have been a fitting last goodbye. Tears rolled down her cheeks and she was overcome with sorrow. She stood and wailed to the sky, crying for her father, her mother and for Tee.

The sun rose in a clear blue sky. But the Gulf did not reflect that blue as it stretched to the horizon. The brown waves came in and out. She knew that the Gulf would be there forever and that her father and now Tee were a part of it. She hurried to join the others at the church for the feast.

A week after the storm the sun rose again in a cloudless sky. Water had evaporated in many places and wet houses and damp earth steamed in the early September warmth. The opening of school had been postponed because of the flood and Martha was impatient, anxious for Miss Boudreaux's return. More than ever she wanted to go to high school, and she hoped that her teacher would help. But school had been delayed yet another day for the cleanup. The islanders called the cleaning "flood harvesting." Martha thought of it as hard work.

She pulled on her heavy boots and looked to see if

Titay was ready to go. "Granma, yo head scarf ain't right. Heah." She retied the scarf, stood back to look and smiled. She hoped Titay would be pleased with her concern.

But Titay only said, "Girl, le's git."

With sticks and buckets, they joined the noisy crew. The men moved fallen logs and heavy limbs. The women and children cleared up smaller things. Everyone looked for fish and other creatures that could be used for food. Martha stayed close to Titay. Her grandmother was slow, but she worked hard and was careful to avoid snakes. The odor of warm mud and seaweed, and of dead plants and animals, was mixed with the scent of magnolia blossoms, giving the air a moldy heaviness.

Shellfish, frogs and turtles struggled in the mud. Frog legs would make a delicious supper. Martha dropped one frog after another into her bucket.

"Watch that snappin turtle," Titay shouted to Martha. "If he gits hold you, he won't turn loose til lightnin flash!"

Martha frowned. "Aw, Granma," she said.

"Aw Granma, nothin; jus let one git hold on you n you see."

Martha had a strong desire to let the turtle snap her just to prove that what Titay said was not true. Instead, she poked the turtle with her stick and watched its feet and head disappear into the shell.

If she put the turtle in the bucket it would eat the crabs and crawfish, so Martha waited until a leg appeared from under the shell, then she slipped a strong string around it and tied the turtle to a bush. It would be safe there until she took it home to make turtle soup.

Sticks beating the bushes for dangerous cottonmouth snakes resounded again and again. A member of the crew screamed in terror before killing a black snake that had slithered out of its hiding place. Some black snakes are not dangerous, but this was no time to take chances.

The hardest part was burying dead rabbits, armadillos, chickens and rats—animals that had tried to swim in the flood, but had become too exhausted to survive. Seaweed, leaves, branches, bark and moss had to be swept into big holes and covered too. Martha worked without stopping.

At last the gray light of evening settled in, and the workers gathered their sticks and buckets to go home. Martha and Titay counted their harvest: six frogs, two turtles and nine crawfish, but only two crabs.

While they prepared supper, Martha peeled onions, chopped the cayenne peppers and cooked the rice. She felt another talk with her grandmother was coming and she dreaded the time when it would begin.

They ate in silence. Even though the frog legs were tasty with rice cooked with tomato sauce, Martha ate little. There was so much on her mind that only Titay could settle. Would she ever go to school again? Perhaps Titay would let her go if Miss Boudreaux would ask.

Just as they finished supper, Titay said, "When you gon start in thinkin bout yo quiltin?"

Martha was now angry at herself for not setting the tone of their conversation. She was not ready for that question.

"I don't know, Granma."

"Whatcha mean, don't know? You mus know. Yuh already foteen n some. That's late fuh a girl not t' know bout portant matters."

"I thought we say we'd wait, Granma."

"We? I never thought that, no."

"But Granma . . ."

"You's sayin wait. Word's still out that you's wantin t' leave this island. Can't yuh see, you can't keep puttin off yo quiltin and the village keep thinkin Cora lie."

Martha wanted to bide time. Miss Boudreaux would be there the next day to open school. She wanted to talk to her before she gave in to showing a quilt pattern. "I got so much t' learn that yuh teachin me. Can't we wait jus a while longer?"

"You's learnin good, yes, but Mat, we can't wait too long. Beau's a good man, hard workin. Men ready t' marry git married. They seem t' be fuh carin bout the woman willin. So I say, girl, yuh can't wait too long."

"I won't wait too long."

"And you member now, foteen slip mighty quick int' fifteen, and 'fo yuh know it sixteen is sebenteen."

Martha said nothing. If only she could find a way to escape the all-seeing eyes and all-hearing ears of the people on the island. Ever since she had been born, they had been looking to see what she was about and now they were waiting to hear that her hand was out for marriage.

She went about clearing the table and washing dishes, determined to put off the quilting as long as she could.

Martha got up early the next morning without feeling rested. She was too excited to stay in bed. Miss Boudreaux would arrive today to open school. Martha had decided to be among the first to greet her.

Pink feathery clouds were high in the silvery sky as she hurried down the trail to the Gulf. The dew, heavy on the brush bordering the trail, chilled her legs.

Would Miss Boudreaux be happy to see her? Would she think Martha could succeed in high school? Martha wondered how she would ask her teacher about going away. The closer she came to the edge of the Gulf the more nervous she became.

The water was still high and the Gulf was restless, but Martha knew Miss Boudreaux would come.

"Mornin," she said shyly to the men and few boys who had come to help the teacher land and unload her supplies.

"Fine mornin, yes, Miss Mat," one of the men said as they all greeted her in turn.

Martha stood apart clutching a shawl around her shoulders. Soon a small speck came into view, and before long Miss Boudreaux's boat came in close to land. From a corroded anchor abandoned on the shore, the boys tossed a heavy rope to Miss Boudreaux. She steadied her boat and waded ashore.

"Martha, my dear," she said. "How nice. I didn't expect you here." She removed her wading boots and supervised the unloading of the supplies. Then she and Martha walked together toward the center of the island.

"Mr. Ovide told me about Tee. I'm truly sorry," Miss Boudreaux said. "Was your summer good in spite of that?"

"Yessum." Martha was suddenly shy. She wanted to appear grown-up, but words would not come.

They walked a distance in silence. Men, women and children were waiting for Miss Boudreaux near the chinaberry tree. Martha knew she had to speak up or miss her chance.

"Hep me, teacher," she cried. "I jus gotta go t' high school."

Miss Boudreaux seemed surprised. She stopped and looked at Martha. "Martha, that's fine. Did your grandmother work out a plan?"

"No, ma'am."

"Does she know that you want to go?"

"No, ma'am. Well, yes, ma'am and no, ma'am. I tole er once. But I don't think she blieve me."

"Your grandmother wants to train you to be a good midwife. She's good, Martha, one of the best."

"But Miss Boudreaux, I want t' finish school."

"You'll have to ask your grandmother."

"Please, can't yuh hep me?"

"Martha, that means going away. Your grandmother would have to agree on any arrangement. You will need money and it's late now to start plans for this year."

"But can't we do somethin?" For a moment they stood in silence.

Finally, Miss Boudreaux said, "Maybe I can go on teaching you."

"Granma won't let me come evey day." Martha lowered her eyes and pulled her shawl tighter.

"Oh, not every day. We can set a schedule. I'll give you assignments that you can do at home. Then I'll see you when they are done and you're ready for more."

Martha kept her eyes fixed on the ground. Miss Boudreaux said, "Martha, one day you'll be able to go away. Maybe when you're older."

Martha looked up and smiled. "I'm so much obliged t' you, teacher."

Miss Boudreaux drew Martha to her for a quick embrace. For a moment Martha was breathless, but in that small space in time she felt sheltered.

SEVEN

M ARTHA AND TITAY walked on the trail that led to the Gulf. The bushes along the way were wet with morning dew, and as they came closer to the water, fog clung to the earth in heavy clouds. The only sounds were those made by their footsteps and the surging of the Gulf. They walked in silence through the fog toward the bed of seaweed.

Suddenly the blurred outline of a boat appeared. Startled, Martha stopped, grabbing Titay's arm. Titay said, "What is it, girl?"

"Granma, you see that?"

"See what?"

Was it a ghost ship? Martha had never seen one like it before. The sails were limp and the boat listed heavily to one side in the low tide, close to shore.

"I git a glimpse of somethin." Titay moved closer to the water.

"No, Granma. Le's go back."

"Wait, girl." Titay held Martha's hand, and as the fog passed in and out they saw that it was a real boat.

They looked up the trail. Only a short distance away Martha saw the form of a man, lying face down. "Granma!" She put her hand over her mouth to stifle a scream. "Look, there's a man! Le's run and warn the village."

Titay moved toward the stranger.

"No, Granma!"

"If he dead, he can't do no harm. If he live, he might need us t' hep im."

The man lay in the mud, his wet clothes clinging to him. Titay knelt and turned his head. With one hand she felt the pulse while the quick fingers of the other hand cleared his mouth for easier breathing.

"He breathes," Titay said, "and he shakes."

He groaned as Titay covered his body with her shawl.

"Run, git hep, girl; we got t' git im home."

Martha returned with only two men, Beau, and Ocie's father, Elmo.

"Who's he?" Elmo asked.

"I don't know," Titay answered.

"Then what yuh want us fuh?" Elmo asked.

"T' tote im in fuh care."

"But e's a stranger," Beau said. "How yuh know . . ."

"We know e's our kind," Titay said sharply. "And if

we wash up on 'is sho, would we want *im* t' ast questions, or take us in?"

"Take us in," Elmo answered.

"So we do as much fuh im."

"But I can't take im. I got no room, no."

"Then t' my house."

"But, Granma!"

"T' *my* house!" Titay said again.

Beau glanced at Martha to show sympathy. Martha shrugged and sighed. She whispered to Beau behind Titay's back, "That's jus like Granma, ain't it?"

The fog lifted slowly and drifted out to the Gulf as they carried the stranger on to Titay's house.

"He'll take yo bed, and you can share mine," Titay said to Martha.

Martha didn't object, but she was not pleased with the decision being made for her. She looked at the helpless stranger. He wasn't much older than Beau. His eyes were closed, his clothes were covered with salt and mud and one foot was without a shoe. She knew he was very sick, for his dark skin had a grayish tone and he shook like leaves in the wind.

Titay covered the stranger with quilts, then turned to Elmo and Beau. "Go now and keep still tongues. He mus rest. In time we ast things we need know bout im."

When the men had gone, Titay said, "Mat, sit near im. I go make warm tea t' bring im round."

The whole bed moved under the stranger's trembling body. His head bent backward and his mouth twitched. Martha ran into the kitchen. "Come, Granma, I think he's dyin."

Titay rushed to the bed. "No, jus burnin with fever. Git the vinegar."

Martha and Titay sponged him, using all their strength to get the job done. He responded as if he were being rubbed with ice. They gave him sips of cool water; then he slept.

Throughout the day they watched him and let him sleep. They roused him only for water and to sponge him with vinegar. His fever didn't cool. Late in the night, Titay peeled a white potato and placed the slices on his head, tying them in place with a clean cloth.

"I think he smiled," Martha said.

"That feel good. We mus make im well. Could be the good spirits brung im in place o' one o' our men. We mus save im."

Martha watched as Titay tucked the quilts with tender confidence and knew that, if he could be saved, Titay would do it.

The next morning the stranger still burned with fever. He groaned and turned and tossed. A worried Titay sent Martha into the woods just beyond the chinaberry tree to look for roots and leaves. "If you can't find the fever bush, then bring some magnolia bark."

Martha took her basket and a stick to beat off snakes and rushed out to gather the herbs. Near the chinaberry tree, she was surprised to see many of the women gathered together so early. With voices raised, they were talking to Cora.

As Martha drew closer, all talking stopped and the women turned to look at her.

"Where yuh rushin, cha?" Ocie asked.

"Yeah, where yuh go so early?" Gert asked.

"You don't gi'e me greetin 'fo yuh ast where I go," Martha said. She laughed to hide her feelings.

They all laughed. Then Cora said, "Fine mornin, ahn? Where Titay? She oughta be out gatherin roots and leaves, no?"

"I don't make answer for Titay," Martha said, and walked on.

"Titay make answer t' us, yes, if that stranger bring death t' this island," Cora said.

What if the stranger did have some sickness that would spread throughout the island? Martha wanted to run home and tell Titay what Cora had said, but when she looked back and saw the women huddled together in worried talk, she knew she had to hurry to find the herbs. Titay must make the stranger well.

"How's he, Granma?" Martha asked as soon as she entered the house.

"He know he in the world, but he cry in pain."

"Yuh ast his name?"

"He say a hard one fuh me, so call im Hal. He from up the Mis'sippi River."

"Spose what he got spread, Granma?" Martha asked. The look on Titay's face made her sorry she had spoken.

"Who think sich?" Titay asked sharply.

"The women."

"The women?"

"Cora."

"Gimme them herbs. We break that fever and he live. You see." Titay went to make the tea.

When they had sponged him and given him the tea, he slept in a deep sleep with even breathing.

"I mus make m' rounds now and tend the other sick," Titay said.

"Mus I stay heah lone?" Martha asked.

"I'll send Ocie t' set wid yuh. If he rouses, gi'e im tea or water. But I'll be back directly."

Titay hadn't been gone long enough to attend one person before she returned. "How come yuh back so soon?" Martha asked.

"Trouble. That Cora spreadin evil. They sayin I harbor death. The stranger come t' bring sickness to our people. Ain't that why I found im, they say. No one'll speak t' me. They so scared they won't let me tend the sick. Sayin I might spread sickness to em."

"What yuh gon do, Granma?"

"Make im well! Mat, girl, if he die now I may as well die too, cause Cora's way'll bcome the way of the island."

Martha knew Titay was worried when she went into the room and closed the door to do her communin.

The stranger still slept, his breathing even and quiet. Martha watched his brow and waited for the sweat that meant a fever was broken.

Shadows lengthened and the sounds deepened. Titay stayed in her room, and the stranger didn't awaken. No one had stopped by to talk, to bring Titay little gifts or to ask Titay's advice.

When the waiting had become almost unbearable, Titay began to move about in her room. Soon she came out and bent over the stranger. Then she smiled. "He better, but not best. We'll wrap im in flannel and gi'e im mo tea."

They waited. The moon shone in the small window and cast the shadow of the two women in the darkness over the bed of the stranger.

Finally Titay lit the lamp and said with great joy, "Hallelujah! He sweatin. He be all right. Mat, you go t' bed."

That morning Titay came to her room just before dawn. She said to Martha, "He better. He ast 'Where am I?' and when I tole im he heah on Blue Isle, Lousana, he was sho nuff surprised. Went right on back t' sleep. I know he better."

"Oh, that's good, Granma. C'mon t' bed now and git some rest."

Noise at the front of the house awoke Martha.

"Titay, Titay, come out heah," Cora shouted. "We know you harborin that stranger, tryin t' stroy us all."

Martha jumped from her bed. The sun was high. Cora continued her shouting. "Titay. You in there. Answer me."

Martha was frightened. Had Cora convinced the people of danger? And suppose the stranger did bring a terrible sickness? But he was much better, Titay said so.

She dressed hurriedly and rushed to see if the

stranger was able to show himself to Cora LaRue. "Granma!" she called. "He gone."

Titay rushed into the room. "He can't be." She looked behind the door, under the bed. "He mus be heah. Look see in the kitchen."

Martha ran to the kitchen. He was not there. Other islanders had arrived and Cora was shouting to them. "She got somethin t' hide, yes. If not, whyn't she come answer me? Whyn't she let us see the stranger?"

What had happened to him, Martha wondered. Was Cora working evil tricks? The stranger couldn't just disappear. Martha ran to her room again. He wasn't there. What had happened? She ran to Titay. "Granma, he ain't in this house."

"I'll face er." Titay walked out the door with Martha close behind. Martha was surprised to see so many people standing about in their yard. They were all quiet, but looked afraid. Titay said nothing. She stood, waiting.

"Whyn't yuh answer, old woman?" Cora shouted.

The people mumbled and Martha knew they did not like Cora talking to Titay in that way. But they too wanted proof that their lives were not endangered by the stranger.

Titay didn't answer. She kept her head up, her eyes toward the Gulf. Suddenly a smile spread over her face. Martha looked. The stranger was coming down the path, walking slowly as if he was very tired. He had changed his clothes. He looked worn, but there was a smile on his face. Martha knew that he had been to see about his boat.

Cora might make the people harm him, Martha thought. Her heart beat wildly. "Talk t' em, Granma, now!"

Titay remained silent, her eyes on the stranger. Finally she said, "He's m' answer. The Gulf brung this young man t' us. Le's be thankful fuh the gift."

The stranger stayed on. His boat bobbled on the Gulf at the edge of the island. Martha worried about him. Even though he was better, he was not well. He stayed alone on his boat, and the people still did not trust him.

Each time Martha passed near the place where he was anchored, she wondered what his boat was like inside. What if the stranger needed something? Was he all right there alone?

Maybe she should go aboard and see. Never! *Magine bein lone with a man, not to mention bein lone with a stranger on a boat. Oo-oo, what they'd do t' me.* She tried to turn her mind to other things.

Assignments from Miss Boudreaux were piling up. Titay now insisted that Martha gather certain herbs and seaweeds herself. She had to make the rounds with Titay and sometimes visit the sick alone—especially those convalescing. She helped Titay monitor Cam's pregnancy, which was now well along. Besides, Martha was gradually assuming responsibility for the general run of the house, and for planning and preparing meals. More and more Titay retired to her communin.

One day, as Martha looked for shellfish along the shore, she wandered near a place where the water was deep, but calm. Suddenly she saw the stranger's boat. When had he moved it to this place? He must be feeling much better, she thought.

The boat moved up and down slowly on the water. The ladder was over the side and Martha decided that the stranger must be on the island. What was it like on that boat? She stood still and imagined she could feel the slow rise and fall as the boat rocked up and down. What if she climbed that ladder? But what if the stranger was not on the island . . . ? *I'd be dead sho if Titay found out.* She shuddered.

It was almost noon. All the people would be having the noonday meal. No one would be near the shore. She could climb the ladder and take a look.

Her hands trembled so she could hardly remove her heavy shoes. She didn't know whether she shivered from the water or from fear as she swam to the ladder.

When she climbed up and looked over the sides she was surprised to see a space as big as any house on the island. She stepped over the side and tried to stand. Her shivering and the bobbing of the boat tipped her back and forth, and she almost fell. Then, with her feet almost shoulder distance apart, she felt anchored. She looked out at the solid brown of the Gulf and forgot how frightened she was as she felt the rhythm of the water. A warm glow spread through her as the wind and sun bathed her body.

Then she noticed a collection of bottles and jars of varying sizes. She moved quickly to look more closely. There were small shellfish, eels and plants, and other living things that she had never seen before. She remembered the jars and bottles in Cora LaRue's house. Did the stranger work some evil magic too? Martha's heart pounded with fear.

Suddenly she heard noise beneath her, then footsteps. In her excitement she had not noticed the stairway that led below. Before she could move, the stranger was up on the deck.

"Well, welcome!" he said.

She tried to speak, but no sound would come. Afraid to trust her legs, she crawled away from the stranger toward the ladder.

"I said *welcome.* Wait!"

Martha moved faster.

"Please, wait," he begged. "I'm glad you've come."

Martha saw the smile spread over his face and her heart quieted a little. "What's in these bottles?"

"Oh, that's my work. I'm collecting what we call marine specimens for study of sea life. I hope I'll sell enough to be able to go back to school."

She looked down at the deck and said, "I done a mean thing t' come heah. The people will think you ast me. They'll hate us both."

"Why you say that? You've done no harm."

"But I ain't sposed t' be lone wid a man cause I ain't married."

"Do you believe that?" he asked.

"Heah yuh jus don't do that. That's our way."

They were quiet. Then Martha said shyly, "What name you have?"

"Harold. Harold Saunders."

"You come from far?"

"Pretty far. From Ohio, down the Mississippi River into the Gulf looking for New Orleans."

"Oh, I hear bout that place and the big Mardi Gras. Tis far, yes?"

"Not from here. I was almost there and would have made it, but I got sick. And there was so much fog. I was lucky to land near your island for more reasons than one."

"Strangers we don't see often, no."

"You and your grandmother were kind to care for me."

"Tis her way." Then the fear returned and she said quickly, "I gotta go."

"Not yet. Let me show you the *Marraine*."

"*Marraine*?" How could his boat have that name? "Heah that mean godmother."

"I know. An old sailor from these parts christened it the *Marraine* and that has been a good name for it. It's thirty feet long, ten feet wide and where you're standing now is called the deck."

Martha relaxed a little, and Harold showed her how the boat could be driven by sails as well as by motor. He showed her how to operate the halyard, giving her a quick lesson in lowering sails. She handled the boom and the mast, as he showed her how the tiller controlled the rudder, which directed the boat. Martha was surprised that his boat had two anchors. She had only seen one in operation. One line attached to the front of Hal's boat had an anchor in place.

"Now come below to see my home on water," Harold said.

"No, no," Martha said. "I best go."

Harold, seeing the fear she had shown at first, helped her over the side onto the ladder.

Martha paused and looked up into his face. "M' granma call yuh Hal. You be Hal, yes?"

He laughed and said, "Yes, I'll be Hal."

Martha swam quickly back to shore.

EIGHT

THE NEW YEAR would soon begin. The sun seemed far away in a high sky, and the air was shivering cold. Martha followed Titay on the trail that carried them deep into the woods. She felt no enthusiasm for this excursion. Her mind was on all the schoolwork Miss Boudreaux had planned for her.

She looked back toward the Gulf, and through the trees she could see Hal's boat. The *Marraine* had become a part of the island. Even though the people did not visit Hal's boat, or invite him into their homes, the women greeted him warmly, and the men welcomed him into their circle of talk. Her pulse quickened when she thought of how he, like others, sometimes stopped to talk briefly to Titay.

Presently they came to a wide opening near the

marshland where the earth was soft. The trees on the edge of this place grew tall and strong, with moss-covered branches that hid the sun. The place was dark, cold and damp. Martha had never gone this deep into the woods to gather herbs and roots. She felt that this day in this new place marked the beginning of a ritual—an offering of a gift of some great knowledge. Martha felt uneasy about being the receiver.

Titay stopped at a strange bush. "See this?" she asked, pointing. "Look good now. Then come heah and see this one."

"They like."

"Yuh sho?"

"Look alike t' me."

Titay broke off twigs with leaves from the two bushes. "Now look," she said.

"Oh, they not alike, no!"

"You mus be keen. One's medicine; one's poison. You's gonna have t' know, never guess."

Martha's doubts surfaced and she felt uneasy. "Granma, do I have t' keep all this in m' head? Can't we write it down?"

"T' do this work, girl, take mo'n knowin. Take bein gifted. Tis a way o' livin. Yuh can't do this work wid jus yo hands n mind. You mus have the spirit. If it's writ down then anybody that read could think they know it. This is meant only fuh a few and you one o' em. I'll teach yuh and yo good works'll tract the nex one fuh the mantle t' fall on. You special, Mat."

Martha wanted to cry out, *What yuh mean, special?* She could not keep all that Titay knew in her head.

She had learned a lot from her grandmother, but there was just too much to store in her mind.

Her thoughts kept wandering back to her work at home and to Hal. Would he continue to live on the edge of the island, or would he leave soon? He wasn't like them at all, with his strange clothes, his talk so different and his odd ways, moving up and down shore with his nets, bottles and papers. People wondered, but Martha was not about to explain what he was doing.

As she chopped roots and gathered leaves, she daydreamed about the time she had gone on the boat. There were so many things she should have asked then. . . . Did women where he came from marry at fifteen?

"Mat, girl, where yo mind?" Titay asked. "Fill yo basket."

With the basket filled at last, Martha walked ahead of Titay down the trail back toward home.

Near the chinaberry tree Ocie was enjoying the sun on that cool day. She waited for the younger girls to come to her to take their lessons: to learn to plait hair, to make pillows from moss and to protect themselves and smaller ones from poisonous snakes and plants. Ocie would soon be ready to replace Gert, who had supervised Ocie's training.

"Hey, Mat," Ocie called, "got a minute?"

"I'm busy."

"Gimme the basket and go see er," Titay said.

As Martha walked over to Ocie she churned inside with worry. Seeing Ocie sharpened Martha's guilt for wanting to leave the island. Ocie was satisfied here and the island was at ease with Ocie. And why not? Hadn't she quilted, and married soon after? Hadn't she, as had many women, made her gift to the Gulf?

"Girl, guess what's happenin?" Ocie asked.

"What?" Martha found a warm spot on the grass.

"That stranger gonna stay on. Mebee fish."

"The men won't fish with im," Martha said drily, as though she hadn't given it a thought.

"They will, yes," Ocie said with authority. "They might be usin his boat."

"Who say sich?"

"Oh, tis round."

"That's no proof he's stayin, no."

"The men visit im evey day."

Martha showed no sign of the excitement she felt.

Ocie went on. "The women all say he make a fine ketch of a husband. Mebbe Titay speak t' im fuh you, yes?"

Martha looked up and the frown on her face and the look of anger in her eyes made Ocie say, "But yo hand's out soon, yes?"

"I ain't thinkin bout no gittin married," Martha said quickly. She picked at the grass.

"You will after yuh show yo quiltin patten."

Martha sensed that Ocie wanted to talk, to be friendly. And Martha wanted to talk too, if only to find out what the people thought about Hal. Did they know she had been on his boat? There were so many things she wanted to know, yet she was afraid to ask questions. She might reveal more than she wanted known.

Finally she said, "I gotta go." She didn't look at Ocie as she got up from the grass.

"Wait, you don't," Ocie pleaded.

Martha was tempted to stay awhile longer, but the thought of gossip frightened her. "Yeah, I gotta."

She slipped into the house and went to her room. Now she was angry at herself for not being smarter. Maybe, if she had just listened Ocie would have talked.

In her small room she looked at the walls that were neither papered nor painted. Dots of resin oozing from the pine boards looked like wild honey. Two box crates sat under the little window. One served as a chair and the other was covered with a red cloth. There were seashells and a tiny ebony wood elephant on top of it. The elephant, though old, was still black and shiny. Titay said it was a gift from a man who had come on a boat from the faraway Indian Ocean. Martha looked at these things without seeing them. She was too concerned with herself and what she had to do and with what she wanted to do.

What were her choices? Maybe she could help Miss Boudreaux. Or she could make and mend fishing lines. She could join Beau and his family picking moss. She did not trust herself to prepare remedies from roots, leaves and herbs. She had too much fear and too many doubts.

She lay still and remembered being on the boat. Then she imagined the boat moving slowly, slowly over waves way out into the Gulf. For a moment she forgot the fear, guilt and the misery of her responsibility. Somehow she knew she would leave this place. She would find a way. She would! She went to work on her math problems.

Finishing that assignment made her happy. She went to find Titay. "Granma," she called, "lemme know when yuh ready t' make the rounds."

Each day now, Martha gathered the herbs and made the rounds with Titay. As she bandaged wounds, sponged feverish bodies and learned to treat measles and whooping cough, none of the women would have guessed she worked with doubt of her capabilities.

There was always so much to do. Even now, as she walked to the commissary for kerosene, she felt rushed. The day was special when Ovide brought in new bolts of cloth and thread. Often on that day he gave a necklace, earrings or some other trinket to the first woman who made up her mind to buy a piece of cloth.

Today was one of those days. The women were already waiting outside the commissary when Martha came along. They were all talking at once. But when Martha appeared, the chatter ceased.

"Mornin," Martha said, to break the silence. "Mr. Ovide must bring many surprises tday, yes? He be late." Ovide came by pirogue, from the same little town where Miss Boudreaux lived, bringing mail and other commodities each day. He went home the same way each night.

The women laughed in anticipation and Ocie said, "You pick yo dress t' wear t' nounce yo quiltin, ahn?"

Martha sensed meanness. *That's all they think bout—me gittin married.*

"Oh, she'll be makin a fine one, eh, Mat?" Gert said.

"And that she deserves," Alicia said, "with all the fellows waitin t' scramble fuh her hand."

There was laughter, but Martha said nothing. She wished she had waited until later to come for the kerosene. She had too much on her mind for chatter about cloth, thread, quilting and dress patterns. She was about to go home when she saw Hal walking down the path from the Gulf.

He wore his shirt open at the neck and held a long stem of grass between his teeth. Martha had forgotten how tall he was. Now his glowing ebony complexion underlined his well-being. He seemed in no hurry and though he was too far to hear the sighs and stifled giggles of the women, he walked as though he knew he was being watched.

Martha pretended she was not even aware of Hal's coming. But she quaked inside with the secret she and Hal shared. The women must never know she had been on his boat.

"Oh, that stranger. Ain't he fine?" Alicia said, and winked. Even though Hal was now accepted by all, they still called him "the stranger."

"A fine ketch if ever I seed one," Gert said.

"Lucky fuh Martha she could have the season's first quiltin." Ocie teased.

"He'll ask fuh her hand, yes," Alicia said, and all the women laughed.

Hal came toward them and greeted them in his deep voice, which still sounded foreign. "How are things this morning?"

The women giggled and answered together. "Fine mornin."

Then to Martha, Hal said, "And is your grandmother well?"

Martha dared not look at him when she answered, "She well."

Just then Ovide came to open the commissary and the women rushed inside.

Ovide had brought three bolts of new cotton to choose from and, for the one who chose first, a small mirror, but Martha was not surprised when no one rushed to buy.

"A lil mirror like that in *my* house, never!" Alicia said. "Too easy t' break. And when it breaks that's seben yeas bad luck."

"Good Lord, seben!" Ocie cried.

"Yuh better cover a mirror when it storm, and when somebody die too. If yuh don't they soul'll be trapped in that mirror and the mirror'll sho turn dark," Cora said.

"Too much trouble. No mirror fuh me," Alicia cried.

The women's talk upset Martha, but she was more irritated by the twinkle in Ovide's eye and the satisfaction he was getting out of the women's talk. *I'd gladly take that mirror. But mebbe breakin it might bring bad luck. But how?* She remembered Titay covering their mirror when it stormed. *How can a mirror do all that? Mirrors don't do nothin but reflec.*

The women's fear and the smirk on Ovide's face humiliated her. That humiliation turned to anger and before Martha knew it she shouted, "Tis stupid t' think that bout a lil ole lookin glass."

The women gasped and Ocie said angrily, "Miss Know-It-All . . ."

"Pay er no mind," Cora said. "She blieves that. She can't be hexed by nothin, that girl. She already been hexed through and through, bein bo'ned in a stom."

The other women said nothing, but the hostility on their faces was frightening. They turned, almost as one, and left the commissary.

The mirror was still lying on the counter when Martha went to pay for her kerosene. But before she paid, Hal walked into the store and Ovide went to get his mail.

"I'm glad you're still here," Hal said. "I want to give you something. You and your grandmother. I owe you two my life, you know."

Martha was still frightened.

"What about a nice head scarf for your grandmother, and what would you like?"

"Oh, I don't know," she said, still visibly upset.

"What's the matter?"

Had he heard her and the women? She looked at him. Believing he had not, she said, "Oh, nothin."

"Would you like that mirror?"

Regaining control, she said, "Yeah, but Granma . . ."

He grinned affectionately, "Does she think, maybe, you'd spend too much time looking at yourself, is that it?"

Martha did not answer and he said, "I know I enjoy watching every move you make. Do you know how beautiful you are?" He smiled and looked into her eyes.

Martha's face burned and her scalp tingled. She averted her eyes from his smile and intense gaze. Without looking at him, she said, quietly, "It might bring us bad luck."

"Where I come from we call that superstition. You're not superstitious, are you?"

She looked up at him. "Mebbe."

"Here, take it. It won't bring bad luck, I promise."

"But Granma . . ."

"She doesn't have to know. If you don't tell, I won't." He whispered, "Don't fear the mirror, fear *fear* of the mirror."

"Say what?"

Hal repeated what he had said and they both laughed. Then he took his mail from Ovide, paid for the head scarf and the mirror and gave them to Martha. "Tell your grandmother to wear this in good health, and you take care now." He left to join the men outside the commissary.

Martha covered the mirror with the head scarf so no one would notice. She glared at Ovide as if to say, "I'll show yuh, I ain't scared o' no mirror."

Should she tell Titay about what had happened with the women? About the mirror? No! Not about the mirror. Titay might make her take it back. She'd be careful, and no one need know.

At home she went immediately to her room. She

placed the mirror in the space between the floor and cloth-covered box crate.

That evening, she made sure the mirror was still in place. Maybe she shouldn't keep it. If only she could be sure that what the people said and thought were *not* true. Would having the mirror keep her from going away? And what if Hal told? *We sho gittin a lotta secrets.* Suddenly she felt frightened. But he wouldn't tell. Maybe he was right, but did even he know?

She opened her small window and looked up at the evening star that twinkled in the sky. "O, Lord," she said aloud, "how come I ain't wise?"

NINE

MARTHA got out of bed noiselessly. She carefully turned the wooden latch to lock her door. When she stooped to pick up her mirror she waited a moment. The silence told her she was right; Titay was still asleep. Quickly she removed the mirror and turned it to different angles so that the reflected sunlight played around the room.

In the light from the window, her dark skin glowed with tints of deep brown and red. She thought of Hal and how he had looked into her eyes. A warmth from deep inside sent a smile spreading over her face. What if Titay saw her smiling like that? Carefully she stored the mirror in its hiding place.

Dressing slowly, she heard voices from the front of the house. Titay said, "I come, right away." Then she walked quickly to Martha's door and knocked. "Git ready, Mat, that baby's on its way heah tday."

For the last few weeks they had spent lots of time with Cam. Only last week they had readied bedding for the birth. Sheets had been washed, boiled in a lye solution, ironed and carefully wrapped to keep them sterilized.

Martha's hand trembled as she buttoned her blouse, and she had trouble tying her head scarf. She was anxious, excited, uncertain with feelings of joy, then fear. What if things did not go right for Cam? Should she tell Titay about the mirror? Titay might not let her go if she knew.

"Hurry, girl," Titay called.

Cam was waiting. She had already put the carefully wrapped bedding in the oven to make sure it was still sterilized. Martha got busy helping the father feed the children before they started out to his sister's house. On Blue Isle, the mystery of birth was for the eyes of women only.

The bed was made ready for Cam. Water was heated. Cotton and wool to wrap the baby in and the sterilized goose grease were put in place. Titay sat in the room with Cam while Martha finished a few house-keeping chores. Then Martha waited in the kitchen, reading for a history test.

Suddenly she realized how still the house was. No sounds came from the room. She thought of the mirror. Had something gone wrong? Things could go wrong, that she knew. Martha remembered the story she had been told of how her mother had died when she was born on that stormy night. Titay had been forced to make a terrible decision: would it be Martha or Martha's mother who lived?

Martha trembled, charged with happiness that she was alive. That feeling changed to guilt and then to deep sorrow that she had never known her mother. She scolded herself for thinking things could go wrong. Cam was healthy. Titay had watched over her diet, her exercise and knew every stage of the unborn baby's development. Yet Martha prayed that all would go well.

She tried to concentrate on her assignment, but her mind wandered with worry.

At last Titay came for her. "Come, hep me now. That lil one's on its journey, so be quiet and still."

The curtains were drawn and the room was lighted by a lamp at the foot of the bed. Martha saw Cam's face drawn in pain, but no sound came from her lips.

Titay whispered, "Hep yo chile, chile'll hep you."

Cam's breathing and Titay's whispers became one rhythm. The room was very quiet. Martha heard her heart beat as she watched the two women. Cam grabbed Titay's hand and held on. Titay gave of her strength.

Soon Titay whispered, "Now." Martha saw that the baby's head and shoulders were coming. Titay placed a finger under each little arm and lifted the baby up.

The baby let out a cry and Martha said, "It's a boy."

"Sh, sh!" Titay whispered as she clamped the cord and carefully placed the baby face down, his arms and legs folded, on the mother's belly. He rested there.

The baby was so quiet Martha felt something was

wrong. She held her breath. She wanted to say, "Do something, Titay," but Titay just waited.

Cam's hands touched her baby lightly. Martha watched Cam caress the small dark body against her flesh and thought of the waves of the Gulf touching the shore. The mother's breathing was the only sound heard in the room. Suddenly the baby moved. First an arm, then a foot, then he quivered; he breathed! Titay smiled. Her face in the lamplight brightened and she looked young.

The strange quiet, the baby's movement, the mother's breathing, Titay's smile—all these things touched Martha. She stood still, her eyes unable to turn away. A slow rising surge of joy passed through her. It stayed for only a second. She had never known such joy and was saddened that it could not last.

With swift precision Titay cut the cord that connected the baby to its mother. Until now Martha hadn't really seen Titay's hands. What beautiful hands, wrinkled with age, but soft and sure. How gently they touched that baby as she cleaned him and wrapped him in the layers of cotton and wool to keep him warm. Then she sent Martha for Cam's husband.

When they left the happy mother and son, Titay said to the father, "Leave em lone awhile t' git quainted and t' rest."

In the twilight of day, Martha looked at her grandmother. She was an old woman now, tired after her day's work. But as if she knew what Martha was thinking, Titay said, "Tis joy, Mat, t' bring one o' them lil ones safe through that dark t' light and life."

TEN

"You hurry back heah and don't come sayin you weary, yuh hear me?" Titay called as Martha rushed out of the house. She went along the path that led to the school.

"Hey, cha," Ocie called. "Yuh goin like a house afiah. Ain't got no time fuh yo friends no mo, ahn?"

"Hey, please don't say that, Ocie." Martha was surprised that Ocie would even speak to her after the scene at the commissary.

"Ain't it true? I sho don't see yuh. Always uner the teacher. I got some news, but go on. Our way ain't good nuff fuh yuh."

Stung by Ocie's tone, Martha felt trapped between the women and Miss Boudreaux. Between the old way and the new. But she must hurry. She would be late and Miss Boudreaux would probably chide her again.

If only she could go away to school and have the time she needed for her studies. It was all finally coming together for her. Lessons with Miss Boudreaux and what she was learning from Titay were clearly related. Words she wrote in her composition book were like the words Hal spoke. What if she spoke like that?

She wished that Ocie was still a friend. Then she would have someone to tell that the teacher was always surprised at how well she did algebra; how much fun she had seeing things in her science book that she knew already; and that the things about the earth, water, light and animals that she did not know, she found exciting to learn.

She wished her teacher could understand why it was so difficult for her to talk words that she wrote. What would the women think if she went around saying: *I do not ... he does ... she is ... you are? That I'm crazy,* she thought. Then she remembered Ocie words: *... got no time fuh yo friends no mo ... you always thought you better'n us.* She knew she would never talk book talk in front of those women, no matter what Miss Boudreaux said.

Miss Boudreaux was waiting. Martha tried to appear calm as if she were not late, but her hands perspired and her stomach churned. She gave Miss Boudreaux her algebra assignment first.

"You did all these?"

"Yessum. They come easy, teacher." She breathed a sigh of relief. She was not considered late.

Miss Boudreaux kept her longer than Martha had

hoped, insisting upon language drill. Martha resisted learning something that she would never use. She thought it was a waste of time.

As she prepared to leave her teacher she was filled with mixed emotions. Part of her wanted to give in to the way of the island and part of her wanted to give in and talk and act like Miss Boudreaux.

She gathered her books and papers and took leave, feeling the teacher's kind but questioning eyes upon her back.

Miss Boudreaux called to her. "Martha, I believed you when you said you wanted to finish high school. I think you can. You'll soon be in the tenth grade."

A smile spread over Martha's face. "Me, teacher. Tenth grade!" She covered her mouth to stifle a shout of joy and ran from the room.

The house was filled with laughter when Martha got home. Women were in the kitchen and the smell of fresh coffee sent out a warm welcome. Everyone seemed to be talking at once. Martha longed to burst in and shout her news, but she slipped into her room to listen instead.

"Magine me a granma!" Gert said.

"Oh, I hope yuh do git a boy baby as fine as yo Tee was," Alicia said.

Oh, Lord, Martha thought, hitting her head with her fist. *That was Ocie's news and I didn't listen.*

"How fur gone is Ocie?" Martha heard Cam ask.

"I don't know, but Tee be drowned since September," Gert said.

"She could be fo months, or mo," Titay said. "You tell that girl she better git heah to see me, and fast."

"What's wrong with these younguns waitin so long t' tell?" Alicia asked.

"Chile, I don't think she knowed. Commence tellin me she feel funny. Like nibbles inside, and I look and she spreadin aready." Gert laughed.

Martha continued to listen, wishing that she had not gone to see Miss Boudreaux but that she had stayed and talked to Ocie. *So Ocie's pregnant,* Martha thought. Her mind ran to Tee and she wished he were alive.

"Ain't Ocie had no mornin sickness?" Titay asked. "No dry heaves?"

"Naw. She ain't had none o' that, no. Strong lil ole woman that Ocie be, and just turned sixteen."

"How old Mat now, Miss Titay?" Cam asked.

"Fifteen, next birthnight."

"That girl better git on with er nouncement. What y'all waitin on?" Alicia asked.

Martha's scalp tingled and her hands began to perspire. She strained to hear Titay's answer.

"She all wrapped up in this heah work now," Titay said. "But yuh know Mat. Take er own good time. We see. But tell that Ocie she better git heah. She late aready."

"Yeah, she be den-thick with that Cora lately," Gert said. "Jus hope she ain't thinkin bout Cora midwifin er."

Miss Know-It-All. . . . Our way ain't good nuff fuh yuh. . . . Surely Ocie would not risk going to Cora.

Martha thought of Cora's attitude toward Titay and Titay's way of midwifery and felt a sense of alarm.

That night, Titay and Martha shared a light supper and cleared the dishes with almost no talk. Martha wanted to ask about Ocie's pregnancy. When had Ocie become den-thick with Cora? Surely Ocie knew that Cora was not a true midwife and that to waste time was a great risk. . . . There were other questions she wanted to ask, but she recalled the women's words about her quilting and decided she had better not risk getting Titay onto that subject. She excused herself and went to her room.

The wind came in sweeps and gusts. Dark clouds raced in the sky, playing hide-and-seek with a full moon. Before beginning her assignments Martha stood in her window watching shadows come and go as the moon peeped through darting clouds. Low laughter mingled with voices of people passing, some stopping briefly to talk to Titay in the front of the house.

Finally she settled to her work, wondering if the reward would be worth the labor. She thought of her teacher, so different from her grandmother. If only there was some way to be proud and happy in Titay's way. But there were other things that she must know, see and do. She wanted to know how Titay's herbs worked and why. Titay only knew they worked and that was enough for Titay.

Why couldn't that be enough for her? She fell upon her bed, her head buried in her folded arms, fighting the rising frustration.

"Miss Titay, anybody home?"

Martha jumped from her bed, her heart pounding at the recognition of Hal's voice. She couldn't understand the feeling of excitement that Hal's presence always brought since that day in the commissary when he had looked at her. The warmth that had spread through her then often came at the sound of his voice. But she didn't want anyone to know that, especially Hal. Why had he come?

He had been coming by more frequently, staying longer just to talk. Martha was always surprised at how much Titay had to say to him. Titay was known as the great listener, but with Hal her words overflowed.

"Where do you hide your list of all the herbs you use?" Hal asked.

"What yuh mean, lis?" her grandmother answered.

"I name and label all the things I find here and keep a record in a book too, so I'll know what I have."

"I ain't got nothin like that, no," Titay said, and laughed.

"But how do you know what you have and how to use it?" Hal seemed truly surprised.

Titay laughed again. "So t' write make it true, ahn? I got it heah in m' head. I know how t' use it from m' heart.

"I learnt m' trade heah but I thought I need know mo. So I went out there. I learnt a lot. But I seen plenty meanness and sufferin in lean-tos fuh my people near them main hospitals. The peoples woulda been better off at home. That's when I cided t' come on back heah and take care folks in they own houses."

Titay, quiet for a moment, sighed and said, "I jus

wish Mat'd unerstand that I can teach her all she need know right heah. Cause I done learnt a lot heah too. Nuff t' know ain't nothin new uner the sun."

Martha listened and felt pride and shame simultaneously. Her grandmother had great wisdom; but could she teach Martha all that Martha needed to know? Some of the things Titay believed Martha could not understand: bad luck mirrors, snapping turtles—children born to trouble in storms. She longed to go into the front of the house and join the talk, but a young woman could not join in conversation with her parent and a young man unless called to do so.

"How bout a lil tea?" Titay asked.

"I'd like that very much."

"Mat, Mat," Titay called.

Martha felt a shiver of excitement.

"Mat, you sleep in there? We got compny. Put water on."

Martha hurried from her room and quickly prepared hot tea. Small thin tea cakes for occasions such as this had been greatly diminished by the women earlier that day. But there were still enough.

At the kitchen table the three of them drank hot sassafras tea with cream and honey. Titay and Hal talked. Martha listened, her chest crowding all the way into her throat with happiness.

Yet there were so many questions crowding her mind. How could her grandmother have gone away from the island and not understand her longing to go? If only she could say to her: *You went. How come I can't go and see fuh mahself?* The urge was so strong, she jumped up from the table and moved to pour herself more tea.

"I'm glad yuh cided t' stay awhile heah," Titay finally said.

"I'm glad I found this place. I could be working near New Orleans and never know it exists. The water around here is a rich source. I like your island."

"You are not afraid?"

Titay shot a glance at Martha.

"Should I be?" Hal's voice was so calm, Martha felt doubly ashamed. Ashamed that she had asked such a stupid question and that she had embarrassed her grandmother by using Hal's language. Looking down, she said, almost in a whisper, "O' sto'ms?"

"I have a shortwave radio that tells me about storms out in the Gulf. But you know, sometime wind and rain can come up so fast it isn't reported. Those storms can be violent too."

"Them's what we call squalls," Titay said. "They come fast n gone jus as quick. Gotta watch em. They can be mean."

All too soon, the evening grew late. Titay saw Hal to the door and said goodbye. Before Martha had finished cleaning the dishes, Titay was in bed and Martha was alone with her thoughts. *Why did I ast that stupid question? Tryin t' use his talk? Titay paid tention too, but said nothin. Never do that again. Hal's smart. Know so much. That's how come Titay like im, talk t' im so much. If only she'd see that I can't take her place til I learn somethin. Til I know.*

The moon, having won over the clouds, shone

through her window. Martha lay on her bed. The rhythm of the Gulf seemed to regulate her breathing. She thought of Hal on his boat, living right on the water. She remembered a time when she had seen the moon as a gleam of light shimmering on the waves. In a rush of joy she hugged herself, and in her own embrace fell asleep.

During the next weeks Martha spent her days working with Titay and her nights poring over her lessons, listening to the calls of the wild geese and the rumblings of the Gulf. In the late-night silence that came in between those sounds her mind wandered to Ocie, who had not yet come to see Titay. Tee loomed in her memories. Thinking of Tee aroused thoughts of Hal, and loneliness fixed itself into her life.

The rumors about Ocie were disturbing. Martha often found herself listening to Gert and Alicia pleading with Titay to talk to Ocie. Martha wondered about Titay's response—that the patient chooses her caretaker and that a good caretaker goes only when called. What if Ocie didn't call?

She watched the closeness of Cora LaRue and Ocie with alarm. The two were everywhere together. The women said Cora had hexed Ocie so that Ocie could not come to Titay. Martha knew better. Ocie wanted Cora because she knew that Martha would come to help with Titay and Ocie did not want Martha as midwife.

It was also rumored that Cora LaRue had hexed Martha so that Martha would never have a quilting.

She would dry up and die an old maid. The women said Cora would prosper and take Titay's place.

But Martha no longer allowed herself to be trapped in the net of questioning: when the quiltin? When the hand be out fuh marryin? In the dying days of winter she was at ease.

In spite of the women's gossip, she was happy. A certificate to prove that she was ready for tenth grade was her proudest possession; and her work pleased Titay and the women. It was as though her world and time were in a delicate balance.

ELEVEN

Now it was summer again—the sun was shimmering. Greens of the earth and the deep blue of the sky gave a lushness to living things along the shore. Martha often felt that the warmth that made the earth sing with life sprang from deep within her.

She felt herself growing, changing: her long lean body now rounding, softening, her breasts no longer buds but blossoms. She needed no reminding: she knew she was a woman.

Often she felt tight, tense inside like a drum's skin; and then again she felt free, roaming in the woods alone, imitating the songs of the birds, dancing with the rhythm of the waves and the wind in the brush. Sometimes, her appetite gone, her nights sleepless, she still bounded around with a burst of energy, her skin glowing, her eyes bright. Titay often asked if she were feverish. Couldn't Titay see that at times she was so happy that she could burst, and at other times she wanted to dissolve in tears?

She knew Cora was frantically trying to win the women's favor, even if she had to do it with fear. Sometimes, even now, Martha shuddered to think that Cora might have led the dance at the fishing festival.

But as much as Martha respected her grandmother's ways and her grandmother's concern for everyone, she sometimes wished Cora had won. *Then I wouldn't feel so tied down t' the peoples' care. I'd be free from it all n long gone. Oh, I need somebody t' hep me t' know what t' do.*

She felt like bounding around the room—the small space was stifling. She rushed out and got her basket even though her mind was not on gathering herbs. She left without telling Titay that she was leaving.

Martha ran to the edge of the wood beyond a place where she and Titay often gathered herbs. This path was seldom used. Tangled with deep green vines and fern, it led to the secluded place where Hal's boat had been moored for a thorough cleaning.

The bushes pushed against Martha and pulled at her skirt. She tapped the ground with her stick to scare off snakes. Even though she knew the area well, she was afraid.

Maybe she should go back. But if she did, she would not have a chance to see the boat before the islanders were through with their noonday meal. Then she thought, *Why'm I so took wid this boat?* She remembered the day Hal had asked if she knew how beautiful she was. *Can't keep my eyes off you. . . .* Now she felt the longings that she could not understand when she heard his voice. Her heart raced and she felt a sudden rush of shame. She wanted to watch Hal in the distance as much as his boat. She hid her basket and hurried on.

The leaves, ferns and brush were so thick in this place she could hardly see the small path on which she walked. It was not good to be alone on this trail. What if a snake bit her and no one was around to help?

Her pulse throbbed and she found breathing hard. Should she go back? Was someone following her? Now she almost ran, and the moist heat made her sweat. The dampness, mixed with the strong smell of flowers, green creepers, dead leaves and brush, made her more aware of danger, but she went on, deeper and deeper into the woods.

A noise startled her. What if she were seen here? She could not say she was collecting herbs without a basket. *I ain't got no business heah,* she thought.

She ran on toward the Gulf. The brush thickened again, but she was not so afraid now. Only the stillness bothered her. No birds sang, no frogs croaked, she saw not even a butterfly on the wing.

Her heartbeat quickened at the loud pounding of the waves. Then she saw the Gulf. And from where she stood it looked like all the water in the world.

Anchored away from the shore, Hal's red and green

boat shone against the brown water. And on the top of the hull *Marraine* had been repainted in bold black letters. The boat was clean; its sails were up. Martha's excitement increased as she watched the boat rise and fall on the waves, the ladder on its side touching the water.

Still careful, she moved in the brush so that she could look up shore, then down. Away down the shore the men who had been helping Hal were taking the trail home for their noonday meal.

Then she saw Hal on deck waving goodbye to them. *How well he gits long wid the men,* she thought. They had never accepted another stranger as quickly as they had Hal.

Alone, with the *Marraine* a distance from her, she listened to the pounding waves as they washed around the boat and rocked it back and forth in its moorings. If only Hal would go back to Ohio and take her as a passenger on the boat. But when would he be leaving? She should ask him. . . .

Martha was so involved in her daydreams, she did not notice the rising wind. In the distance thunder rumbled, and sailing clouds had covered the sun. It could be a squall. Heavy rains, thunder and lightning could make the Gulf treacherous. She must get home.

She could not go back the way she had come. Lightning among trees could be deadly, the flooded path could hold dangerous snakes. And if she were on the trail close to the water, waves could wash her out into the Gulf. But she could run faster on that trail close beside the Gulf and there would be no trouble with animals. Still, she would risk being seen by the men on their way home. What could she do?

The wind came in gusts. Martha decided to risk the trail near the shore. With her head down against the wind, she moved closer to the Gulf. Thunder crashed overhead and green lightning flashed. The wind was now so strong she feared she would be blown into the water. But on she went, not knowing how, and almost not feeling the sting of the mud and brush. The wind whipped her without letup. The thunder still crashed and lightning flashed again and again as the Gulf roared angrily.

Now every step was a struggle, but she could not stop. There was nothing between her and the raging water and the wind of the squall. Then she was at the place where the *Marraine* was anchored, away from the shore. The big black letters stood out against the dark of the Gulf and the sky. Huge raindrops splattered the land and water. "God save me," Martha cried.

In an instant she knew she could take shelter on the boat—but Hal was on the boat.

The raindrops passed and suddenly there was a lull in the wind. The good spirits had protected her, Martha thought. For a moment she watched the *Marraine* float on the water and remembered the day she had climbed the ladder and gone over the side. Then she knew she should not have paused. The gray clouds opened and the rain poured down. The Gulf slashed up over her and she was washed off the path. Martha panicked. She tried swimming back to land, but the wind, the rain and the Gulf were all against her.

She let the waves carry her to save strength as she tried to reach the *Marraine*. What if she was washed past it? She must keep her head and not be so afraid! She bobbed on the waves and reached for the ladder. The sea was so rough that she missed. She rode the waves and reached out again. She must get on the boat or be washed away. Again she tried. Her hands caught hold, and she climbed up onto the deck.

She shivered, drenched with rain and the water of the Gulf. The roar of the wind and the Gulf hurt her ears. Through the pouring rain she saw Hal trying to lower the sails. The boat rocked up and down on the waves. "Hal!" she cried. "Hep me!" Her words were drowned in the wind.

Martha felt sure the sails would be blown overboard and washed away. Waves slashed over the boat and flung Martha back and forth, the salt water stinging her nose and eyes and burning the cuts on her body.

The boat shuddered and creaked, pitching in the wind. Then Martha saw the anchor line disappear, and the boat headed toward the shore. If the boat smashed it would be splintered.

Before she could get her balance Hal was shouting orders to her to save the sails. He rushed to start the motor to move the boat out into the Gulf.

The wind whipped the sails and Martha knew they would be blown·into the sea. Hal screamed directions, but with the loud snapping and cracking of the sails, Martha heard nothing that he said. She hung on to the halyard with all her strength. Her hands, burning as though scalded, bled, but she still hung on. Finally she lowered the sails. The boat raced shoreward with the wind. Martha watched, desperately afraid it would smash—they would drown! Suddenly the motor sputtered. It roared, and the boat lurched away from the shore.

The loosened sails fluttered and Martha had an idea. She began stuffing them into the opening of the companionway that led below.

Faster and faster the land seemed to be moving away from Martha. Her heart pounded with fear. She had sought refuge on the boat only to be washed over the horizon. Fighting against the wind she looked at Hal and she saw that he was in control. He shouted to her to release the anchor line attached to the front of the boat.

At the bow of the boat she pitted herself against the full blast of the driving waves. Pressing her body against the railing, she held tightly with one hand while the other searched for the anchor release. She prayed she would not be washed away. Finally, the anchor slipped into the water and Martha clung to the railings, praying the anchor would hold.

Thunder rumbled in the distance. Waves washed up in a spray now and the wind was no longer a roar. Martha lay next to Hal on the wet deck, exhausted.

He squeezed her hand and asked, "How did you get here?" Before she answered, he said, "Oh, I'm glad you're here. I'd have lost the *Marraine* without you."

She told him how the squall had driven her on to the boat. Then she was quiet, glad that Hal was quiet too. She listened to the waves as they rocked the boat back and forth, up and down, and she felt a oneness with the boat, the brown Gulf and the sky. Aware of Hal beside her, she was filled with a quiet, peaceful joy. Her mind flashed to the day Cam's baby had been born, to the quiet of that day and the unexpected joy she had known with Titay and Cam.

Then she recalled the recent howl of the wind and roar of the Gulf. She looked at Hal. With his eyes closed, he seemed as relaxed as she felt. She placed her other hand over his and let it stay. Finally she said, "Mebbe a child bo'ned in a sto'm *could* be bo'ned t' trouble."

"What?" He raised up to look at her.

"See, heah they say I'm bo'ned t' trouble cause I was bo'ned in a sto'm. I saw this birth and it was so quiet. Evey time I said somethin, Granma said, *Sh, sh.* I was thinkin yuh can't say *sh* t' a sto'm. So mebbe in noise like that I am bo'ned t' trouble, no?"

Hal chuckled as if embarrassed by her openness. "Could be. We're all born to some trouble, especially if we're different."

"Yeah, like m' friend Tee. He was bo'ned t' drown, so people say. And he did." She explained about the hole in Tee's ear.

An amazed look came over Hal's face and Martha was not sure he believed her, but when he spoke he was serious. "Oh, that. I've heard of that superstition. Strange, it's different in every area. In Texas, some people believe that little hole means you have extra senses, can predict the future. That little hole is a pre-auricle pit. It means nothing, Martha, but a little skin missing. Lots of people have it—it's quite common. Listen, what we believe is often what we get."

"I git so scared cause these people round heah blieve so much I can't understand it all. Like m' granma . . ."

"But your grandmother knows so much, Martha. And she has a lot to teach anybody."

"I know. And I like knowin all the things she say, yes. But I can't keep em all in m' head, no."

"Write it down."

"I tell yuh, I can't put all that stuff tgether. I wanna leave this place."

Hal rolled over on his stomach to face her. "Why would you want to leave a place like this? It's so beautiful, quiet and peaceful. There's so much to learn here."

Suddenly she knew she was talking too much and that she had been on this boat too long. She jumped up and moved to the bow and stood looking out toward the horizon. Happiness returned as she remembered that once before she had stood there and felt the wind and the rhythm of the waves. Then there was a sudden revelation: *Mebbe I'm bo'ned t' trouble, but I ain't evil.*

The world came closer and she felt at ease, at peace with herself.

"Martha." Hal came and stood behind her. He slipped his arms around her waist and drew her backward to him. Her heart beat so wildly that she hardly heard the whisper in her ear. "Did I upset you when I asked why you want to leave this place?"

"No." She moved out of his embrace. She could not look up at him, nor could she say to him all that she wanted known about why she must leave.

He reached out and lifted her face so that she looked into his eyes. "Don't be upset with me."

"I ain't. You see this place wid two eyes, so you see much that is good and beautiful. I see wid one eye. I have t' see mo'n this place 'fo I can know if it's what you say."

He laughed and drew her to him. "Oh Martha, my serious Martha. I'll do all I can to help you go. . . ." He held her close. His firm tenderness frightened her and she stiffened. Then he softly kissed her forehead. His lips lightly touched her closed eyes. When he kissed her mouth, all the happiness in the world seemed centered in her heart. She wanted to hold onto him and that happiness forever. Then the fear returned and she broke away. "Please take the *Marraine* in closer, yes."

Nearer the shore she knew she should leave the boat; still, she lingered. Again he held her face in his hands and moved to kiss her lips. Quickly she turned her head and his lips brushed her cheek. There was an invasion of yearning that she had not known, ever.

Martha, pulling away, ran across the deck, down the ladder and swam to shore.

Martha hurried along, following the Gulf trail that would take her home. Gray clouds rolled swiftly. She watched her shadow appear, disappear with the sun. She could not remember ever being so happy. Hal would help her go away! Then the church bell tolled, calling the people together. Had something happened to Titay? Martha's step quickened with fear, and she moved as fast as she could along the trail.

As she neared the village she heard voices.

"Heah's er basket she hid in the woods," Cora said.

"Why'd she hide er basket?" Titay asked, alarmed.

"I tell y'all she was headin tward that Gulf, deep in the wood."

"Where there ain't almost no shore?" one of the men asked.

"Where women that spects our way never go lone," Cora said.

The women raised their voices in disbelief.

Cora had been in the woods. Did she see Martha go near the *Marraine*? Did Cora know Martha was on that boat? Noise rose from the crowd and Martha knew the women were again divided between Cora and Titay. For the first time since leaving the *Marraine,* she felt guilty.

When the crowd saw her there was a great hush. Children looked at her and moved closer to their mothers. Suddenly she was painfully aware of her bleeding hands. Her clothes were dirty and dripping. Her body ached and the scratches on her arms and legs still stung from the salt of the Gulf. She touched her head scarf. It too was wet and half undone.

Everyone stared at her as if she were a stranger. How could she tell she had gone on the boat to save her life? She looked at Titay. Titay seemed so old and frightened. She looked at Martha, but Martha felt that Titay neither saw nor recognized her.

"Look at er," Cora shouted as she approached Martha and faced the crowd. "Where she be in all that wind and rain? If she be clectin herbs like the old lady say, she could reach home befo the squall. Would she clect herbs thout a basket? Ask er—where she be?"

The crowd mumbled nervously and Titay lowered her head. Cora looked at Martha and shouted, "Let er tell us where she be so we can judge ourselfs if she be not the brazen one we blieves er t' be."

The people waited. Martha wanted to run to Titay and tell her not be ashamed, but she could not move.

Then Cora said, "She got a ready tongue t' say we stupid cause we know the power of mirrors. So let er speak now."

Martha remembered that day. She knew the trouble Cora had caused with the women about her wanting to go away. She trembled. She wanted to tell the women what had happened. She wanted to say how she had helped Hal save the boat, wanted them to know what she had felt: a moment of joy in a quiet place, and a oneness with a boat, water and sky. She thought of that moment and could not hold back the smile.

"Look at er," Cora shouted. "She's a brazen, conni-
vin one in league wid the devil."

Martha turned toward Cora with tears in her voice.
"I'm not brazen, no," she cried. "I had to go on that
boat."

Titay, moving toward Martha, said, "Mat, quiet
yuhself."

"Un-hunh! She be on that boat. She connived t' be
lone wid that man. There's mo t' this heah girl n meets
the eye," Cora shouted.

Titay faced Cora and said, "Fiah on the tongue can
make blind the eye. Le's cool down now."

"Yeah," Gert said. "Mat's safe and that's good.
Where she be is fuh Titay t' handle. Le's go t' our
houses."

Martha entered her house very much afraid. Titay
had listened to Cora's accusations. Martha did not
know what to expect.

"Go clean yuhself," Titay said.

Martha bathed and Titay helped bandage her hands.
"You rest and I bring yuh warm tea," Titay said.

Titay came into the room and stood while Martha
sipped the warm liquid. Finally Titay said, "Now I
want yuh t' tell me, what was you doin on that
boat?"

"I woulda drowned, Granma."

"Who you think blieve that? You dare go n be lone
wid that stranger . . ."

"I done no harm."

"You poke fun at our way, callin people stupid. You

: : *112* : :

fused t' have yo quiltin, and now yuh go gainst the island."

"I tole yuh, I woulda drowned."

"What yuh doin way down there by that Gulf when you oughta be clectin herbs, anyway?"

Martha did not answer.

"Say somethin, woman. Why's you at that boat?"

The "woman" frightened Martha. She felt she was being abandoned. "I didn't plan it, Granma, no."

Titay moved to stand over Martha, who sat on the bed with her eyes cast down. Martha had forgotten how intimidating her grandmother's strength could be. Now Titay's voice rang clear. "You denied our way. Yuh done shamed evey girl and woman on this island. Yo punishment'll be sufficient." Titay started toward the door.

"Granma," Martha cried, "don't leave me."

Titay looked at Martha. Martha saw the anger in her eyes. Titay said firmly, "I got no mo words wid you. Yuh on yo own. The island'll deal wid you."

Martha paced her small room. Without Titay's support she had spoiled her chance of going away with the islanders' blessings. She had done what she had to do and what she had done now weighed heavily upon her. She felt all alone. But she was accustomed to being alone. Hadn't Titay set her apart?

The stillness in her house was more than she could stand. She felt trapped in her grandmother's silence.

If only she had made friends with someone. Had not been so busy and neglected Ocie. What would the women think if they knew she had been on that boat before? She thought of Hal. . . . What if they ran him away from the island because of her?

She lay on her bed, restless, remembering the ugly confrontation with Cora. "But I did what I had t' do," she said aloud. Suddenly she felt a calming sense of peace and fell asleep.

She awoke when Titay knocked on her door. "Dress yuhself and come heah," Titay said.

Evening had come. Martha was surprised to see Hal sitting with Titay in the front of the house. She felt embarrassed and ashamed. How long had he been there? What had he told Titay?

Suddenly she wanted to flee—never to see him again. She buried her face in her hands and shook with sobs.

"Martha," Hal cried, moving toward her.

Titay stepped between them. "Yuh done done nuff harm."

"I don't know what you're talking about," Hal said.

"You been heah long nuff t' know our way. We don't go t' the well less we ready t' drink."

Martha burned with shame and Hal said, "We did nothing to be ashamed of."

"You was lone on that boat. In the eyes o' our people that's nuff." Titay looked at Hal and her voice sizzled in almost a whisper. "You done shamed the Dumas name. Disgraced us on this island. Now you be a decent man. Marry er n save her honor.

Hal sighed, jammed his hands deep into his pockets,

lowered his head and hunched his shoulders. "I care for Martha. But I had assumed all along that she was at least nineteen. Martha's considered a kid where I come from. I'm a bit old for Martha. When Martha was born, I was already seven."

"I don't care!" Titay said. "When she be twenty-five and you be thirty-two, won't make no diffunce."

"Well, I guess we can get married."

"No!" Martha screamed. "No, no, I'll not marry im; I ain't marryin nobody. I'm leavin this place." Again she broke into tears.

Titay took Martha in her arms. "Hush," she said. "Hush up and come t' yo senses."

TWELVE

THE ISLAND was divided. Each eye and each ear was an antenna that picked up every gesture, every word. Rumors raced back and forth between those who supported Cora and those who supported Titay. There was agreement on only one thing: Martha had denied their way.

The church bell sounded for the evening services. Martha did not want to go, yet she dared not stay away. When she and Titay arrived at the church, the people had already gathered. The women greeted Titay, but none greeted Martha. Ocie, now only weeks away from labor, barely nodded to Titay before she and her mother joined Cora.

Martha and Titay sat together. Titay joined in the

singing and clapping while Martha sat subdued, her bandaged hands in her lap.

Finally it was time for the testimonials and prayers for the sinful. One by one women and men rose to ask for prayers for forgiveness and for strength so that they would sin no more. Martha was there in body, but her mind was far away.

"There is a sister in our midst tnight who's sinned," the prayer leader said. "Her sin can be fogived. She can be cleansed in the blood and made white as driven snow. She need only come, confess, repent and cast er-self on the altar."

Martha sat still with the amens and hallelujahs all around her. Suddenly she knew it was she who was being asked to repent. She stiffened, the rising anger trying to find space inside her.

"She know who she is. Come, come, sister buke the devil and deem yuhself."

Martha felt crowded with guilt and shame, and for a moment she wanted to stand and cry aloud for forgive-ness. *But fuh what?* Her shame and guilt turned to anger. She stared straight ahead as if contracted, petri-fied. Voices, pleading and condemning, flowed over her. She sensed Titay trembling beside her and knew tears were flowing down her grandmother's cheeks. Still she could not bring herself to move or speak.

The service ended and the members left, their stares burning in Martha's mind. She walked home, shoul-dering her wounded dreams, wondering how she would ever redeem herself and leave Blue Isle with her grandmother's blessing.

Martha slept late. She woke with a start. The silence around her was like that in a deep cave, and for a moment she thought she was still asleep. Then she heard the Gulf, like the heartbeat of a giant, coming through the momentary silence.

For days now no one had come or passed close to their house. Titay would remain in her room most of the day. At twilight she would walk down to the edge of the Gulf. Martha grieved for her grandmother and wished she could undo the shame she had brought upon them.

Martha lay still, thinking it must be almost noon. Her mind told her that she should eat, but her body rejected food. She was full all the way up into her throat. *What a fool I was. Never shoulda gone that far jus t' see im.* She tried to bring back the warm feeling she had known when Hal gave her the mirror; to recall the sheer joy on the boat, but all that came was a feeling of shame. It had been so wonderful, and it had turned so ugly.

In her mind she saw Hal as he had been the last time she saw him—hands deep in his pockets, his shoulders hunched. The shame crowded in on her again. *How could he say he'd marry? He knowed I wanted t' leave this place.*

She remembered that he had said he would help her go away. But how could she face him again? Did he now think, like some on the island, that she was brazen, without manners, conniving? No, she could never look at him again. *How could I be stupid nuff t' think he liked me? Never shoulda gone t' the Gulf. Then nobody'd knowed how I felt and it coulda last foever.*

She sighed and looked at her rope-burned hands. The swelling was gone, but they were still a little sore. Titay demanded nothing from her, and Martha was grateful she could stay indoors, mostly in her own little room.

How would she face the cold stares, the ugly whispers and the self-righteous indignation of the women? She knew well what was in store. The silent isolation meted out on Blue Isle was worse than flogging. Maybe she should have repented, asked redemption and been restored.

Noise from nearby houses—the sound of singing mixed with the rattle of dishes being washed—let her know the meal was over. Martha turned out of bed and opened her window wider. Then she heard movement in the front of her house and footsteps coming toward her room. She scrambled back into bed.

A knock put her on guard. She did not answer. She raised up just as Titay peered in the room. The look on Titay's face forced Martha out of bed. "What is it?" she asked in dismay, taking her grandmother's arm leading her to the bed.

"And t' think I brung er in this world. She talk t' me like I'm a ... oh." Titay's breathing came in gasps. Martha had never seen her in such state.

"Who, Granma? Who?"

"That girl, Ocie. Called me a old woman ... say I

ain't got no order in m' own house, so I ain't fit to birth no baby o' hers."

The hurt in Titay's voice shocked Martha. "What she mean, no order . . ."

"Tis that Cora," Titay interrupted. "She'll midwife Ocie. All the women gather round er now. Her way is won."

"Don't say that, Granma."

"Tis true. Oh Mat, I'm old and tired."

Martha looked at her grandmother. Her thin shoulders were covered with a worn black shawl. Wisps of white hair showed beneath her head scarf, messily tied. A rush of anguish flooded Martha. Why not ask forgiveness and go back to the rounds with Titay?

Her grandmother broke the silence. "Fogit yo way, Mat. Marry the stranger and take m' place. Don't let Cora put er way on this island." Then Titay was quiet. The silence thickened. Finally Titay pleaded, "Say yuh do it, Mat . . . bring peace to us."

Martha still said nothing. She sat, knowing they were miles apart. Her mind flashed to another time when they had been at serious odds. She was then almost twelve, being pressured to confess her sins and be born again. Martha did not know what that meant and would not confess. Then she had spent nights on the mourners' bench as if she were alone in the world, with prayers and rebukes around her. For days the women, including Titay, avoided her as if she were a leper. Still she had waited. She had to know that some change had come in her and in her world.

But that storm had passed when on faith she had been baptized and restored to the good graces of the island.

Now she felt the tears burning in the back of her eyes and stinging her nose as she realized that she had always been a thorn in her grandmother's side. What would save her this time? She could not rely on faith for she *knew*. She had not sinned. She had acted to save her life and the *Marraine*. That was good. She would not marry Hal. If Ocie and the women chose Cora to deliver their babies that was their right. She would leave this island one day soon, she hoped, with her grandmother's blessing.

Martha was so set on this idea that she was startled when Titay pleaded again. "Say it, Mat, say you'll fogit yo way and marry."

"Granma, I don't want t' marry now. I wanna go way t' school."

"Who fill you wid all this crazy notions? Where yuh git yo ways?"

"From m' own heart."

"Girl, don't yuh know, you can be fooled tryin t' learn yo ownself?"

"Who can I go t', Granma, t' ast things?"

"Tis not our way, t' ast why or what be."

"Ways change."

"You done come t' a lot o' knowin all a sudden," Titay said. "Whyn't yuh say you'll marry?"

"Cause they'll think me a liar. I didn't do nothin wrong."

Titay lost her patience. "Yuh go gainst the island, be lone wid a man and say yuh do nothin wrong?"

"I saved m' life."

"N played in the hand o' the wicked."

"Aw, Granma . . ."

"Girl, don't yuh know yuh can't tear down the walls and the roof o' a house and the ceilin stay? If you don't marry that man you know what'll happen to yuh? Nobody'll want yuh. Who'll want sich a hand? What'll yuh do?"

"In time somebody'll want me fuh what I am. Things change, Granma."

"You's a woman," Titay shouted angrily. "That yuh can't change. A man want a woman that keep *his* way. And where yuh think yuh gon go? Mongst strangers?"

Martha said nothing. The only sound in the room was that of Titay's labored breathing. "Alone and lonely be fuh ole women like me," Titay said as if talking to herself. "Mat, yuh young. Yuh needs arms fuh shelter."

"Oh, Granma, listen, I heah you, yoself, say, 'A woman who got no place t' put er hand fuh support, put it on er own knee!' "

"You say words in the right place, but tis doin the right way that count, Mat."

"You want too much from me, Granma."

"Tis too much t' keep the way? T' marry that man?" Titay sat still for a moment. Then she said, "Yuh know, you think yuh wise, don't yuh? But mind you, Mat, no one wise is wiser'n er own people."

The silence in the room now was more ominous than any that had yet fallen between them.

In a voice full of tears Martha said, "I never thought mahself wise. I only want t' know." She turned onto her stomach and covered her head in her arms. She fought to hold back her tears until Titay left the room.

THIRTEEN

MARTHA dressed carefully. Looking in her mirror she tied and retied her head scarf before settling on a style that gave her a carefree air. All eyes would be on her, and she wanted the women to know she had not lost the will to live. It was time that she got out of the house and it was impossible to live on the island and not see the women and their stares.

When she reached the path that led to the Gulf, the sun was already aglow and the dew fast drying. Martha walked briskly, not knowing exactly where she was going, just that she wanted to get to the water's edge.

She glanced back at the village and was caught in the peacefulness. The houses in rows looked asleep. Black iron pots for boiling laundry were cold now, with gray ashes almost touching their bottoms. A lone child in a white shirt, probably his father's, was drawing water from the outdoor pump and white smoke was rising, indicating the beginning of a fire for the breakfast meal.

It was a quiet scene that belied the feelings of fear and distrust that were now rampant on the island. Martha sighed and turned away, feeling remorse for her part in that fear and distrust. The women needed her for their midwife, but they wanted her only on their terms: just like them—happy keeping the customs of the island.

Martha hurried toward the water's edge. To her surprise, she was not the only one who had sought the comfort of the constant rhythm of the rolling sea. The man's back was to her and at first she didn't know whether to go ahead or turn around. If only he were farther up shore away from the trail. Then she could slip by in the opposite direction and indicate her desire to be alone with the swiftness of her walk.

She stood on the trail listening to the waves, watching him pitch pebbles out to sea with a fast hard throw. She waited, wanting to go closer to the water's edge. She hoped he had as little interest in talking to her as she had in talking to him.

Before she had moved, he turned to pick up more pebbles and saw her on the trail. The surprise showed in his face that was now a golden tan from the summer sun.

"Mornin, cha," he called. "C'mon, I'm leavin directly."

"Mornin, Beau," she said softly as she approached him near the water.

"I often come early," he said. "I feel close t' Tee heah in the mornins."

A sadness flooded Martha. She felt ashamed that she had not realized that Beau would be as lonely and grieved as she was about losing Tee. She suddenly knew how separate men and women were on Blue Isle—and now she was uneasy because she knew if someone saw them there, it would be said that she had connived to meet him.

He must have sensed her distress. "I won't stay, though there is somethin I gotta say t' yuh."

She lowered her eyes hoping that he, unlike the others, would not condemn her.

"Word is out yuh won't take the stranger in marriage. I'm glad. I loved yuh, Mat, since I can remember. I fear, though, you won't consider the likes o' me. But I still care."

It hurt to have him talk this way. She didn't know how to respond.

He went on. "Have yo quiltin and I'll take m' chance." He waited, then started toward the trail.

"Wait." Her eyes on the sand, she said, "I don't think I'll have a quiltin. I don't think I'll marry . . . nobody, Beau."

He started to walk away and she moved closer. "Please. Wait," she said, still not looking at him. "I knowed you liked me, Beau, and I'm glad I got the chance t' hear yuh say it. I hope we can talk sometimes and be friends." She looked at him. "Can we?"

The seriousness on his face eased into a smile. "Oh, cha, of course. We friends."

She watched him until he disappeared. Then she walked along the shore, thinking that she had a lot to learn about the men of her island. She thought of Tee, who had dared suggest that she consider leaving, and now Beau, who, in spite of what some people thought of her, would take his chance when she presented her quilt pattern.

Then she remembered Titay's words: *Who'll want sich a hand? Where you go? Mongst strangers?*

Beau wanted her hand. Maybe she should forget about going to school. *A man want a woman that keep his way.* What was a man's way? What was Beau's way? What if she showed her pattern? Would Beau's father let him bid for a woman who wanted to go on learning? She knew she would take her lessons as long as the teacher gave them. Would Beau laugh and find her crazy if she sometimes spoke like Hal?

The thought of Hal made her angry and Titay's words hit Martha hard: *Mongst strangers?* Would people away from here laugh at her? At the way she talked? At the way she looked? She ran down the shore as if to get away from herself and her confusing thoughts. She ran until she came to the path that led to home through the woods. She slowed as she neared the chinaberry tree. The loud talk and shouts of the women startled her.

"I don't care what y'all say," Ocie shouted. "I know what Mat done."

I jus don't want no Cora midwifin m' granbaby," Gert shouted.

"Tis m' granbaby too," Ocie's mother said.

"And nobody like Mat gon touch this chile. She always thought erself better'n us," Ocie said. "So smart, lordin o'er us. And so uppity with that stranger. They say she leavin Blue Isle. I hope she do."

Martha wanted to show herself to stop the talk, but she hesitated.

"Don't talk sich trash," Alicia shouted.

"She trash," Ocie shouted back. "Let Titay say somethin t' er and see if she listen t' er own granma. Let Titay put er house in order. Tis like Cora say, Mat found somethin new wid that stranger, she'll never be tame. No man'll tame *her*."

"Don't *bring* that Cora filth heah, no," Cam said angrily.

"I ain't fuh fendin that Mat, no, but I don't talk bout Titay," Ocie's mother said.

"Mat er own woman, yes," Alicia said. "Titay can't take Mat's sins on her head, no."

"You bes come t' yo senses, Ocie, girl. That woman Cora no midwife, no," Cam said.

"And no old woman who can't handle er own granddaughter can't do nothin fuh me. C'mon, Mama, le's go." They left, Ocie heavy with her unborn child.

Martha was too ashamed to let the women see her. She stayed on the edge of the woods, listening.

"I fear fuh that daughter-in-law o' yourn, Gert," Cam said. "Cora ain't measure her yet, one time; she eat all wrong, yes. Nothin but sugar cane. No greens, no liver, no oranges. Titay make you eat all them things, yes."

"What Cora know?" Alicia asked. "Bet she ain't even pared good clean goose grease. What she know? Evil spirits hinder birth. So she say put nine bags round the stomach and spread special potion on birthin bed."

"Can't tell that Ocie nothin, neither her mama. They den-thick with that woman, Cora." Gert waved her hands in the air then grabbed her head and cried, "Ocie, too big. She swell up. That's no good. I tell er, see Titay 'fo tis too late."

"She blieve in Cora's magic. Cora tell er no pain," Cam said, and all the women laughed.

"Taint funny fuh Ocie, no," Gert said. "I fear, really fear."

Martha approached the tree and when the women saw her they became quiet, their eyes on her. Martha's heart pounded as she hurried by, her eyes averted from their stares.

Just as she came to the commissary, Hal was walking up the path from the Gulf. He waved to her, but she pretended that she didn't see him, hastening her footsteps. Since the evening she had said she would not marry him, she had kept plenty of space between them.

At home she went directly to her room, not wanting to face Titay. She closed her door softly, hoping Titay would not know she had come. She lay on her bed confused and miserable. *Ocie hate me. Trustin Cora wid er life.*

The silent treatment was getting her down. She closed her eyes, trying to shut it all out of her mind. She knew she had to get away from this place, but she felt empty, dry, lost, with a great desire to go, but no plan.

Suddenly she jumped from her bed and rummaged through the crate that served as a desk. She found pencil and paper and began to write:

Miss Boudreaux, Dear teacher. Please help me go away from here. I will work hard for just room and board and time to go to school. For the sake of my life, I have to go. I thank you very much. Sincerely.

She reread what she had written and wondered what her teacher would think. She looked at the word *Sincerely.* She erased it and added, *Humbly, Martha Dumas.*

Hurriedly she sealed it. She ran out of the house toward the commissary. Ovide was just leaving as she came up. "Ovide, Ovide, please! For the teacher, yes. I be happy for her answer, yes. Please."

She watched him place her letter in his pocket and felt a mixture of satisfaction and anxiety. Now she must wait.

FOURTEEN

THAT SATURDAY NIGHT the moon cast shadows and silhouetted trees. The scent of crushed magnolia blossoms and honeysuckle filled the humid air with an overpowering sweetness. The air was hot and sticky. Moisture clung to Martha and mosquitoes buzzed around her, in spite of smoke rising from rags set to smolder. In the heat and stillness the least noise was heightened.

Drumbeats were heard throughout the island. Laughter and occasional shouts brought the gaiety of Cora's toe-party to Martha's front porch. Martha felt a loneliness tugging at her that she could not dispel. She did not want to go to Cora's party, would not have gone had she been invited; but being treated as if she did not exist was taking its toll. Martha sighed.

It had been more than a week now and no word had come from her teacher in response to her letter. Not even acknowledgement of receipt. It was hard for her to refrain from asking Ovide if he had delivered it. She hoped he had given it to Miss Boudreaux right away.

Now she was more worried than ever that she would never get away from the Gulf, from the woods, and the women who could never understand her longings.

The tempo of the drums increased and laughter and shouts grew louder. Martha worried that the noise might disturb Titay, who had gone to bed earlier. Her grandmother had not been herself since Ocie called her unfit to serve as midwife. Titay's reason for being was to serve.

Martha thought of Titay's pleading with her to bring peace to the island. She felt sorry that she still had not convinced her grandmother that it was best for her to go away. What if she did not find a place? She didn't see how she could say she had sinned, have a quilting and get married. Suddenly she felt that fate had dealt too serious a blow to one who only wanted to know what was beyond this little island.

Sustained shouts and laughter led her to believe that toe-buying was underway at Cora's party. The women, behind a curtain, would show only their toes. A man could choose toes and claim the lady for a dance after paying a price. Was Ocie there? Maybe Beau and Hal were there too, laughing and enjoying the fun. She imagined Beau choosing toes, seeing to whom they belonged, and refusing to buy.

Ocie's large sad eyes loomed in Martha's mind.

Ocie's baby was overdue now. Her hands, feet and legs were terribly swollen and she lacked that glow that crowns many women in the last stages of pregnancy. But Ocie had been grieved, alone and lonely. This thought made Martha sad. She hoped Ocie was at the party having fun too.

It was almost midnight when Martha left her porch for bed. The driving rhythm of the drums, laughter and the rolling Gulf filled the island with a droning sound of happiness.

Titay had already gone to church when Martha woke. It was still hot and sticky; the village quiet was in sharp contrast to the gay sounds of the night before. Martha busied herself preparing the Sunday dinner.

If only there was something to do, some place to go. She recalled how, as children she and Ocie went on long Sunday afternoon walks with Tee and Beau to pick flowers and play games in wooded meadows. What had happened now that they were men and women with nothing fun to do? How did this happen to them? *Too few of us,* she thought. Or maybe it was the way of the island. Could she be friends with Beau without being his wife? Or anybody's wife?

When she had finished preparing the food she wished to escape her hot house and sit in the shade of the chinaberry tree. But she did not want to risk an encounter, especially with the churchgoers.

As she stood in her front door, listening to the waves rolling in and out, she dreamed she was miles away.

* * *

Afternoon crawled toward evening. Titay did not come for dinner. When Martha finally decided to eat alone, the food was cold. Why didn't someone come by to ask for her grandmother, or just to say hello? She sat on the back porch trying to catch a cool breeze, but there was no air stirring.

Then the silence was shattered by a knock on her front door and a frantic call for Titay. Gert was there, in worn house shoes, her hair uncombed.

"Where Titay?"

"She ain't come home all day. Not since church, no."

"Where she at?" Gert cried.

"Yuh know Granma. She could be anywhere."

"If she come heah, quick, tell er Ocie been laborin two days n one night. I want Titay. She mus come." Gert left running, her shoes making a flopping sound.

Two days. *Can't be,* Martha thought. Cora had a party last night. Surely she would have been with Ocie. Then Martha was ashamed of having thought Cora would neglect her patient. Ocie probably had false alarms and there had been plenty of time for Cora to go back and forth to make sure all was well. But Titay was a constant midwife who liked to be completely free when a mother was even near labor.

Big moths fluttered against the screen door. She watched, wishing her grandmother would come home.

Finally Titay came. She greeted Martha and started toward her room. The old heaviness rose in Martha's chest and she longed to cry out to her grandmother. *Care bout me. I can't help the way I am. Try, Granma, you all I got.* But she said only, "Good night, Granma." Then suddenly she cried out, "Ocie need you!"

"I know Ocie in labor. Gert found me."

"You not go?"

"I go if Ocie or her midwife send fuh me."

"It might be bad, Granma."

"Yuh mus know I don't choose. A midwife is choosed; she can't force a mother. If Ocie call, I go."

"But Ocie might not know better."

"In life ignance no excuse. I say t' er, come see me. That I do. That's all. She choosed Cora. I bide by that." Titay went into her room.

When Titay closed her door the house seemed more silent than ever, and Martha felt the full force of her grandmother's independence. Did she have a right to refuse to go unless called? Then Martha remembered the day she had heard Ocie say Titay could do nothing for her. But Cora was not a safe midwife. Women who wanted children did not go to Cora. . . .

Martha lay on her bed in the darkness listening to the familiar sounds that crept into her silent world. *Ocie need her husband,* she thought, and it was hard for her to hold back the tears.

Martha clapped her hands and stamped her feet, urging the couple on. Ocie was dancing the courting dance. She was dancing the part of the man, doing all kinds of intricate steps, turning, twisting and twirling to the beat of the drums. The drums beat faster, then faster, faster still.

Why was Ocie's partner doing the woman's dance? Then Ocie's partner fell down and cried, "Hep me, dance fuh me." Martha knew she must help. She pushed but the crowd held her back. The partner cried again, "Martha, hep me." Martha knew it was Tee and she pushed and shoved to get to him as his voice became louder and louder.

Martha sprang up in her bed, drenched with sweat. Her room was flooded with the light of the moon. She realized she had gone to sleep fully clothed. Remembering the dream, she shivered in the heat.

She lay back down on her bed but could not rest. Finally she went into the front of the house. There were no crickets, no frogs sounding their songs. The quiet was eerie. It was as though nature was holding. The light of the moon cast deep blue shadows and Martha felt that she was alone in the world.

Suddenly there was a long shrill wail that pierced the calm of the village. Martha's heart stopped for a second and then she cried, "Ocie!"

She rushed to her grandmother's door. But before she knocked the door opened. Martha was surprised: her grandmother too was fully dressed. Before words passed between, another unceasing scream broke into cries that filled Martha with anguish and urgency. "That's Ocie, Granma. You gotta hep."

"I'm ready, but they gotta call."

"How can yuh say that? Go!"

"Don't yuh judge me. You learn this now. I can't go. What if I'm not wanted n be in the way? I can't vilate no other midwife. I won't go lessen I'm called."

The cries stopped. Martha stood ready to shield herself from the possible recurrence of the wracking scream. Then came the sound of running footsteps, headed toward their door. The heavy steps were combined with a deep voice calling, "Miss Titay, Miss Titay!"

Ocie's father burst through the open door. "Please come. Save Ocie." Then he broke into sobs.

"I'll come too, Granma," Martha said.

When they arrived Martha was shocked at the lack of concerned activity. Ocie's mother sat in the kitchen, off in a corner, dazed, while Gert sat at the table, moaning softly. Cora rushed from the bedroom where Ocie lay. "Why you heah?" she demanded. "Who call fuh you?"

"I brung er. Now you move out the way." Ocie's father spoke with such force that Cora scurried from the door. Titay rushed in.

Martha gasped when she saw Ocie weakly thrashing, entangled in the bedding. Her eyes were closed.

"Oh, my God," Martha cried. "We too late, Granma."

Titay was already assessing, looking for signs of life. Ocie opened her eyes and tried to speak. Her mouth opened, but no sound came. Her eyes were pleading when she issued a long sigh.

"Le's git busy n save this baby," Titay said.

Martha helped Titay prepare for the delicate but strenuous task of turning and withdrawing the baby from its mother. There was not the usual quiet, tender, relaxed timing. Titay barked orders and Martha obeyed. Then there was a small boy quickly severed from the cord. Titay labored frantically to give him life. "Get Gert," she cried. When Martha returned with Gert, Titay had a crying baby, wrapped. "Heah, hold im in yo arms, caress im now. Touch im, hold im close. His mama's no mo."

Titay turned away from Gert. Martha rushed to her grandmother and took her in her arms and the two women let their pent-up anguish dissolve in their tears. Finally as Titay was leaving, she said to Martha, "Take charge o' cleanin up heah now."

Tears stole silently down Martha's cheeks while her mind raged. She was tormented by angry questions for Cora and the women who had stood by as Ocie moved steadily toward this tragic ordeal. But she had no time now for grief, no time for anger. This one time in her life she was glad for the ritual, and she plunged in to do the things she thought made no sense, things that had never been explained so that she understood.

Quickly she covered all the mirrors in the house. It was urgent that Ocie's spirit depart without its reflection being trapped in them. While covering the mirrors she called for someone to go for Cam, who could serve as a wet nurse. As Ocie's baby snuggled to Cam's breast, Martha was satisfied: he was a strong, eager eater. He would survive.

In no time at all other women were there to help. At first they stood around, skeptical of Martha, wanting to know why Titay was not there.

As Martha assigned duties it was as if she were now trapped in Titay's ways. Her voice and her body movements were alien to her. Step by step, she prepared Ocie's body for the wake to be held that night and for the burial that would follow the next day. Balm oil and spices were mixed for anointing; the winding sheet folded and draped. When the body was laid face toward the rising sun, Martha slipped a picture of Tee and a pair of knitted boots Ocie had made for the baby into Ocie's hands. They would make her journey less lonely.

Then the house had to be cleansed thoroughly. The room in which Ocie had died had to be emptied of all furnishings, the bed placed in the sun for purification and the walls and floor scrubbed. Now the women worked with ease, but with some awe at Martha's efficiency.

"Ain't that girl jus like Titay?" one of them said.

"Lord, that's the sho nuff truth," another replied.

It was dark before Martha was free to leave. People were beginning to arrive for the long night vigil with the dead. Martha was exhausted but satisfied that she had done all the things Titay had taught her—all the things the people believed were necessary to release Ocie's spirit from the house and send it on its long journey.

Ocie's house was filled with neighbors and friends when Martha slipped away home. Titay had left water on the stove for Martha's bath, but Martha was too tired to bring in the galvanized tub and prepare the water. She washed her hands and face at the pump and stretched out on the back porch, ignoring the heat and mosquitoes. Suddenly she was back in her own mind, and she remembered her dream about Tee and the dancing. Her mind filled with Ocie's screams and she felt hopeless. She could now see the faces of the women as they went through the ritual of shrouding. They seemed sorry that Ocie had died, but not a one seemed to understand that the death need not have happened. Anger flared in her as scalding tears burned her eyes and cheeks.

Then she was trapped in a dark place where silence filled the space and touched her every nerve. Yet she could not move, not even twitch, and knew she had to give in to this darkness. She was sinking. Suddenly there was a burst of light. She opened her eyes and the sun was beaming down hot and she was drenched with sweat. She remembered the dream and became alarmed. Maybe her life, like her friend's, would end in this place.

Days after Ocie's funeral the village settled to its rumors. Cora was said to be hiding in the woods biding time to return and take revenge against Ocie's father. Her few followers believed that if Cora had been left in charge, Ocie would have lived.

Martha knew that Ocie's father was out to avenge Ocie's death. She also knew that Cora would never be seen on the island again. Cora had been warned, and on the night of Ocie's wake Ovide ferried her away. Martha did not know where she had gone.

Weeks went by, and rumors about Cora gave way to speculations that Martha would soon show her quilting pattern. Her hand would be out for marrying. Beau and Hal were the two most often mentioned suitors, but there were older men on the island who were said to be hopeful.

When the women met at the commissary or under the chinaberry tree, their talk was about Martha. Hadn't she been most helpful in the preparations for Ocie's burial? Her way had been Titay's way and surely Titay's way was theirs. Martha would make a wonderful midwife and a beautiful bride. There was not enough praise for how she had covered the mirrors when they had believed all along that Martha thought herself above such a practice.

However, as the weeks sped by the women became confounded. Martha moved among them in silence. She spoke only when it was necessary, and often the look in her eyes seem to pass through them without seeing.

The dream of dark silence returned again and again. She often woke shattered by screams that brought her out of troubled sleep to find that nothing in her life had changed.

She began to shrug away thoughts of a response from her teacher and of leaving Blue Isle. Her teacher had failed her as she had failed Ocie. She could not dismiss the idea that if only she had talked to Ocie and warned her, then maybe Ocie would have come to see Titay. She told herself over and over again, *Ocie blieved I thought mahself better.*

Her mind was so riddled with turmoil that she could neither eat nor sleep. Loss of weight made her face small and drawn and her eyes large and unusually bright. But each day she made the rounds, throwing herself into the routine as if she had settled on this as her life's work.

Martha often caught her grandmother looking at her worriedly. With a hand lightly on Martha's shoulder, Titay would shake her head, but say nothing. Martha felt that her grandmother was giving her plenty of time, waiting for her to open up and share what was on her mind. She longed to tell Titay about the letter and her doubts and hopes. Yet because she had not heard from her teacher, she was glad that Titay didn't ask questions.

Then one day she stopped by the commissary to see if there was any mail. When told there was none, she burst into tears. She bolted out the door toward the trail that led to the Gulf. Then she stopped, angry at herself. Why had she put all her hope and trust in Miss Boudreaux? She should have known better. Why would her teacher think that someone like her would succeed away from the island? No young person she knew had ever left that place except by death.

She recalled the day Ocie died. It had been easy to forget all the questions, all the doubts, and act like Titay—to do things the way the women wanted and expected them to be done. There was no uneasiness, no fear, no one reminding her that she had been born to trouble. That day she had not been trouble's child. She had been one with them: one of their own. They had been joined in that ritual with only one thing in mind: the passage of Ocie's soul on its journey.

That day had been easy. But did she want the easy

way? She cupped her face in her hands to stifle the sobs. Suddenly she was blocked on the trail, and looked up to see Hal. She turned to flee, but he grabbed her wrist and held her.

"Listen, I'm fed up with your treating me like I'm the enemy. Why are you doing this to me?"

She was surprised at the tone of hurt and anger.

"If you're upset because I said I'd marry you, I'm sorry. I didn't know what you had told your grandmother."

She remembered that day. The humiliation she had felt returned and she was angry. "Yuh coulda ast."

"Do you know what it's like facing your grandmother? The only thing I could think of then was doing what *she* thought was right."

Martha laughed. "So you didn't want t' marry, no?"

By the change in his expression she could tell he had said more than he wanted her to know. She said, "I don't think you no enemy."

"You won't believe this, but I was on my way to ask your grandmother to let me talk to you. I finally got news about schools for you."

"I don't need no news bout schools. Too late fuh that."

"What you mean, too late?"

"I ain't goin nowhere."

"Why did you change your mind?"

"Cause o' Ocie. If I'd never said I was gon go way, mebbe she'd come t' Granma and be live tday."

"Oh Martha, you don't believe that, do you?"

"Whyn't she come? I know. Tis cause she blieved I thought mahself better'n her."

"Oh Martha . . . I . . ."

"She tole me so erself."

"That's no reason to think you caused her death. Even if she had come to Titay, things could have gone wrong."

"I don't know. But I can't fogit I didn't try t' bring peace after I went on yo boat."

"I don't see how anybody can blame you. You're being too hard on yourself."

"The women, they don't seem t' know that it needn't happen atall. Oh, if only she'd took care erself."

Hal sighed. "Hey, listen to the news I brought, okay?"

"If you wanna tell it."

He told her about schools of nursing and midwifery in places not too far away from the island. "Now you'll have to finish high school."

"I tell yuh, I ain't gon go, no. They need me heah. They want me, yes. So I'm gon stay."

"Martha, when you told me you wanted to see this place with two eyes, I thought you meant you wanted to go away to learn some new things. That you wanted to give to the women here some other ways of looking at their lives."

At once Martha knew that was what she wanted, though she could not have said it that way. And there was nothing she could do about it. There was no one to help her even finish high school. She looked at Hal. "When I said that I thought I could, but I can't now."

"But you must! Can't you see they need to know that maybe Ocie should not have died? If you stay here, Martha, how will you help them? You'll settle in their way and become comfortable knowing nothing more than what's here. I was so impressed with your wanting to be different. Don't give that up."

How could she tell him that she had no one to turn to. She knew no place to go and she had depended upon her teacher with no results. She lowered her eyes and said nothing. There was a long silence. Finally she said, "When I said that, I really blieved I could. I can't now."

"I'm leaving the island, Martha, soon."

She looked at him, pained. "Oh, yuh have t'?"

"Yes. I hadn't planned to tell you that today. But I'm going back to finish school. I want to be a marine biologist. I rented the boat to come here to collect those things and now I think I have enough money to get my degree."

Martha felt a sudden loss. "So I won't see yuh, no?"

"Change your mind and come to Florida for nurse midwifery. I'll help you all I can."

She thought of her teacher and the letter: *For the sake of my life.* She held her bottom lip between her teeth, trying to hold back the tears, but they splashed her cheeks.

"Come on . . ." He took her hands and held them firmly. "It's not that bad. We'll find a way."

She looked up at him and smiled. She knew what she had to do. Reluctantly she withdrew her hands and hurried back along the trail.

At home, Titay called, "Mat, come heah. I was waitin t' tell yuh, I'm gon invite the village soon t' nounce yo quiltin. You's fifteen and a bit mo. We ain't gon wait no longer."

"But Granma . . ."

"Now you listen. Yuh done proved yuhself good. I mus say I never thought you'd make the woman you's made. I'm glad t' gi'e yuh up fuh marryin."

Martha sighed and said nothing.

"Now I'm gon call the women. We gon git this quiltin on, yuh hear me?"

What could Martha say? Maybe she should be grateful. Titay would show her pattern and she'd be married. She was weary of going against her grandmother when she had nothing definite to back up her own will.

FIFTEEN

THE AUGUST SUN beat down on the island with a vengeance. Sweat poured off Martha, leaving her limp and without energy, but life went on. She did her house chores, made the rounds and listened, sometimes laughing, when the women teased her about her impending engagement. As the time drew closer, Martha became more tense inside, but she moved as though she was unconcerned about the plans Titay and the women were making.

Two days before the showing of the quilt pattern, it was so hot no one wanted to stir, indoors or out. Martha was up early, but because there were things to do to ready the house for the announcement, Titay left to make the rounds without her.

Martha hemmed and pressed her dress. She had a strong urge to try it on, but it was just too hot. She stretched out on the floor in the front room to take a break. She must have dozed, for she was startled by loud knocking and shouting at the front door. "Anybody home?"

Martha raised up. Hal was standing at the front door. She was so surprised that at first she didn't know whether to let him in or pretend she was not at home.

"Wake up," he called.

Then she realized he could probably see her through the screen. Why had he come? Uncertain, she moved slowly to the door.

"I have something for you. Ovide sent your mail."

Martha rushed through the door and took the envelope from his hand. Quickly, she read the return address. She was so excited she had trouble opening the envelope. Hal helped her open it.

"Here, tell me what it says, Martha."

"Read it. Read it t' me. I'll jus die if she say no."

"You read it."

"No, no, tell me."

"Read it!" he said, shoving the letter into her hands.

Her hands shook as she read: *Dear Martha, I am sorry that it has taken me so long to answer your letter. But you are a special person and I wanted a special place for you. I have found that place in New Orleans.* Martha let out a yell and threw the letter in the air. She wanted to laugh and cry at the same time.

Hal picked up the letter and continued: *A doctor and*

his family will take you. You can help them in their home and maybe sometime in his office, earning room and board. Your schooling there in the city will be free. They do ask that you find a way to get to New Orleans.

"Oh Martha," Hal said. "I'll take you. That will be a good reason for me to visit the city."

Martha could hardly contain herself when Hal left. She was going away! Should she tell Titay now or wait? What if Titay said she couldn't? She became frightened. She had to go. She would not let Tee and the women down. And how would she face her teacher again if she didn't accept that offer? But how could she tell her grandmother? She rushed to her room and hid the letter where she was hiding the mirror.

When Titay returned, Martha had finished her chores and cooked dinner. She felt tense inside, but she served the meal and ate her food as though nothing had happened.

After they finished eating, Titay asked to see the hem in her dress. Martha shyly displayed her work, her heart feeling squeezed in her chest.

"Oh, but you gon look good. I see no way yuh won't git ast t' marry."

Martha carefully folded her dress. "Granma . . ."

"Yeah, Mat."

"Aw . . . nothin." She just couldn't break her grandmother's heart.

In spite of the rain, the August night was hot. The windows were closed, but moisture seeped in. The house had a musky, mildewed smell. Martha sat next to Titay sewing covers for the backs of two cane-bottom chairs. Titay was busy finishing the interlocking circles on Martha's introductory quilt. The only sound was that of driving rain.

Finally Titay said, "I worry bout yuh, Mat. You don't seem like no woman bout t' nounce a quiltin, no. I hope yuh ain't still mournin Ocie."

"Don't worry, Granma. I'm mebbe tired."

"Tain't natual fuh a young woman t' be so sad. Tis that goin way, ain't it?"

Martha did not answer. She had never told her grandmother that she was planning to go away as soon as she found a place. Now that she had a place to go, and with the party the next day, she didn't know what to do.

Of course the women had assumed that Martha was pleased with the plans for the quilting announcement. Cam was making herself a new dress; Gert had agreed to make cakes for the occasion and Alicia promised homemade ice cream.

Martha kept her eyes on the needle. As she made small neat stitches her mind was filled with Titay's question. She couldn't bring herself to tell Titay about the letter, and she couldn't embrace the thought of marriage now to anyone on the island. What if she had married Hal? She would be going away with him to Florida. . . . She burned with shame. *How could I think o' marryin im jus t' go way when I was so mad when he gi'e in t' say he'd marry me?*

She was startled by Titay's voice. "I think yuh scared o' marryin. You think yuh won't be happy? Nobody happy all the time. The thing is t' be happy mos the time. And that yuh be in marriage if yuh don't look t' yo mate, but t' yuhself."

Martha put the sewing down and fled from the room. The rain blew in and washed her face as she stood looking out of her small window. The night was pitch black. What was she going to do? That letter had to be dealt with!

After a time she closed the window and went back to the front room. Titay sat as if waiting for Martha's return.

Martha wanted to cry out, "Can't yuh see, I ain't happy one bit. Call off this quiltin." But she picked up her sewing and said, "Granma, I'm all right."

"Fine," Titay said. "I jus wish sayin made it so."

The rain beat against the house and the Gulf boomed in the distance. The sounds that had often brought a sense of well-being to Martha now underlined her unrest.

The rain passed. The sun rose aflame. There was still a lot to do to finish readying the house. Martha, nervous, anxious and afraid that Titay would notice her unusual tension, worried that her grandmother would never get out on her rounds.

"Mebbe this front room oughta be rid o' eveything cept chairs, cause we gon have a crowd heah tnight," Titay said proudly as she started on her way.

Martha hurried to slip the neat new covers over the backs of the cane-bottom chairs. Cam was coming to braid her hair with fancy white beads. But there could be no hurrying in that hot still air. She felt weighted down, and even though she was drenched with sweat, Martha felt no relief from the heat.

Time was against her. How could she dare let all those people come to hear that there would be no quilting? If only her teacher were on the island. Miss Boudreaux could explain how important it was to go away to school. The people would listen to her. *Why don't Cam come on heah?*

Floors had to be scrubbed, but she put that off and filled oil lamps for all the rooms. Just as she was about to wash the lamp chimneys, Cam came bounding up the front steps.

"Thought I wasn't gon come, didn't yuh? Well, I'm heah and I gotta hurry back. M' dress fuh tnight ain't even finished so le's git started right now."

Martha was glad for the necessity to sit. Cam's fingers on her scalp relaxed her.

"You sho got some pretty hair, girl. When yuh marry, wear it down n loose. Yo husband like that, yes. Now I'm gon make this real pretty n all the fellas gon be wantin yo hand, what yuh bet?"

"I don't want all o' em wantin m' hand."

"Don't kid now. We all like them looks from fellas that turn our world all red and gold."

"Cam, what's it like bein married?"

"It's all right."

"Jus all right?"

"Oh, yuh know. At first tis jus fine. Sorta like when yuh little and yuh stretchin yo mind with the mail order catalog. Member how we useta stretch our minds buyin all that stuff and ain't had a dime? Girl, you do some dreamin when yuh first git married. Then the babies start coming."

Martha felt Cam's mood change with the clutch of her hair, but she said nothing.

"And they keeps comin n yuh wanna stop em n yuh don't know how. Then evey month them icy claws of fear git fixed in yuh and then it ain't good. I'm talkin too much, ain't I?"

"Naw ... I ast yuh, didn't I?"

"Well, it ain't all that bad. Sometimes things happen and you sorta stretch yo mind again. Like when the stranger come heah. I betcha evey woman on this island got t' thinkin n dreamin. He had come from somewhere that ain't heah, so our minds got t' stretchin."

Martha laughed. "Yeah, even Granma talked mo'n she ever talked befo."

"Yeah, it ain't all bad. But girl, now like you, you smart, Mat. Marryin might not set wid you like it set wid me. I'm stuck."

Cam sighed and Martha felt the resignation in her fingers as she worked the last beads onto the braid. "Oh, that sho look good, if I have t' say so mahself."

Martha crossed to the front room mirror, "Oh, yeah!"

"But you oughta see the back, girl."

Martha rushed from the room and returned with the small mirror Hal had given her. She held the mirror so that she could view the back of her head.

"Mat!" Cam cried. "Ain't that the mirror Ovide brought that day?"

"Sho is," Martha said, matter-of-factly trying not to show her uncertainty about Cam's attitude.

"How'd you git it?"

Still trying to act unaffected, Martha replied quietly, "The stranger gi'ed it t' me."

"Oh, girl, it sho ain't brought you no bad luck."

They bent with laughter and Cam said, "I gotta run, girl, and feed them babies n finish m' dress."

When Titay returned she beamed at Martha. "Cam did yuh up good. Yuh look like a woman ready t' offer a proud hand."

"Granma," Martha said almost in a whisper, "I want you t' tell em tnight that I'm gon go way."

"*What?* Mat, girl, yuh know, you's a puzzle and a vexation. Why yuh always gotta break the spoke in the wheel? N done waited til the last minute."

"Granma, I jus knowed mahself I would go."

"I knowed it. All the time you's settin round heah with yo face all long, and I ast yuh if it was that goin way. Then yuh let me go head and vite the island. Now tell me, where yuh think yuh gon go anyhow?"

Martha read the letter to her grandmother. "Granma, please say I can go and gimme yo blessin."

"What if I say yuh can't go?"

"You wouldn't say that, Granma, cause yuh know I have t' go."

Without saying more, Titay left and closed herself in her room.

Martha put away food, washed dishes and scrubbed the floors. Sweat poured off her, but she had to keep busy or fall apart. Her mind was made up. She would go, with or without her grandmother's blessing.

Titay stayed in her room. Martha finished cleaning the lamp chimneys and made them sparkle. She placed lamps around, lighting the whole house.

The guests started arriving as soon as darkness fell. The women brought flowers and placed them everywhere. Gert delivered her cakes and put them on display so every one could see.

"Where Titay?" they all asked.

In spite of the weight of the sparkling white beads, Martha held her head high. She looked composed in her pale yellow dress, but she was quaking inside.

"Where that granma o' yourn?" people asked.

"Yeah, where that Titay?"

What if her grandmother refused to appear, and no announcement was made? Martha knew she could never tell the people that she was leaving against her grandmother's will.

The house filled; people spilled out onto the porch. No one dared miss the announcement that Titay's granddaughter's hand was out for marrying. Why was Titay taking so long?

Finally she entered the front room. Her white hair was piled high on her head and she wore combs and jewelry that Martha had only seen carefully wrapped. Her dress was made of heavy handwoven cotton, the

color of red bougainvillea blossoms. She greeted her
guests, saying, "Welcome, welcome."

Martha had never seen her grandmother so beautiful. She moved in the background to let Titay take
over. She noticed that the men were all gathered on the
front porch. Hal's laughter mixed with the voices of
others.

She went to the back porch to try to get a breath of
fresh air. But it was stifling everywhere. She tried to
think of what she would say if Titay announced her
hand for marriage. "You's a puzzle and a vexation,"
rang in her mind. What would Titay do?

Then Titay was calling for quiet and attention.
Martha went back into the house.

"Go stand by yo granma," Gert demanded.

Martha felt small and insignificant beside Titay,
even though she measured much taller.

"I thought I was gon say one thing tnight," Titay
said, "but y'all know how tis. I gon say another. My
Mat is leavin us t' go t' school."

There were moans and cries of "Oh, no." Titay let
the noise subside. "Now, now, y'all. M' chile ain't de-
partin fo good. She jus gon go t' school, and I'm bout t'
gi'e m' blessin."

Martha was so happy that nothing else mattered.
She let the tears flow down around her cheeks before
she wiped them with the back of her hand.

The people became quiet, and Titay sensed their
mood and said, "Yeah, we hate t' see er go. Tis as
though she sayin she can't be happy mongst us."

Martha's spirit soared when she looked out at Cam

in the crowd. *Me, I'm stuck.* She realized that she was on the threshold of searching, learning, knowing, of stretching her mind.

Titay went on. "But I'm gon gi'e er m' blessin knowin she's a good smart woman. She'll go and she'll see out there what I always say, ain't nothin new uner the sun. All that's new sprang from the old."

Martha looked at Titay and knew. No matter what she learned when she left home, it would be tested in the fire of her grandmother's truth.

MILDRED PITTS WALTER

grew up in Louisiana and now lives in Denver, Colorado. A graduate of Antioch College with a masters degree in education, she has traveled across the United States as an educational consultant and storyteller, and to Africa, China, England, and Haiti as well. The author's novels such as *Lillie of Watts, The Girl on the Outside,* and *Because We Are,* and picture books such as *Ty's One-Man Band* and *My Mama Needs Me* have been widely praised.

In a starred review of her original African-American fantasy *Brother to the Wind, School Library Journal* said, "Walter's writing is imaginative, engaging, and filled with metaphors of flight and fancy and the infinite wonders of life."